STATE OF UNION

KINGMAKER TRILOGY
BOOK 3

PAULA DOMBROWIAK

Dark Angel Publishing

KINGMAKER BOOK THREE

STATE
OF *Union*

PAULA DOMBROWIAK

KINGMAKER BOOK THREE

STATE OF Union

By: Paula Dombrowiak
Copyright © 2024 Paula Dombrowiak

Cover Image: Stock Photo
Cover Design: Lori Jackson www.lorijacksondesign.com
Editor: Hart to Heart Edits
Proofreader: Amy Rooney

CONTENTS

For those who love a reformed playboy.

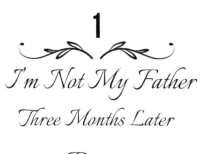

1

I'm Not My Father

Three Months Later

Darren

*I*t feels a bit like coming full circle, standing outside of campaign headquarters.

My campaign headquarters.

Before I open the door, I have to take in a breath.

"You'd think we were building the H bomb," I joke half-heartedly as I walk through the rows and desks filled with people. People I'd never met, and here they are making calls, conducting polls, asking for money and vouching for me as a candidate worthy of representing them in the most critical of matters.

Rausch stands nearby in his perfectly pressed suit having a conversation with one of the volunteers. He's in his element, a comfortableness that I have yet to embrace. There's a flickering loss of self-confidence, like I don't belong here, like all these people have put their money on the wrong horse.

I cough into my hand to get his attention.

"Who are all these people?" I gesture to the bullpen, noticing a blue and white banner with the name Walker hanging on the wall. Not to mention the streamers that hang along with it. The smell of coffee and sugary donuts fills the small, packed space.

"Do you think your father knew the names of each volunteer on his staff? He had better things to do." Rausch leads me into the office at the back that's separated from the rest of the room by a glass partition. I take a seat behind the desk and twirl a pencil between my fingers as I watch the volunteers.

"I think that we should organize a rally…"

I tune him out.

Over the past few months, the campaign has ramped up from just a couple volunteers to a now-bustling room. I tap my chin with the pencil. My mother spent all her time organizing the volunteers for my father's campaign. She knew all their names, even if my father didn't. He relied on her for those things so that he could concentrate on the more difficult matters like how to appeal to voters, determine their wants and needs, reach out for support. Granted, his campaign wasn't for a small district in Virginia, but this is my starting block.

I'm only slightly aware of Rausch's voice in the background. "I have you on the schedule to speak at the VFW hall on Thursday. I think…"

"I'm not my father," I abruptly interrupt him, and he stops talking.

I set the pencil down and look across the desk at him. "It's not a statewide campaign. The problem with Rory Colton is that he didn't know people like Ethel or her neighbors and the problems they faced. It made it easier for him to vote down a bill that could have saved them instead of saving the state money,"

Looking back into the heart of the office I say, "It's a small southern district of Virginia. I need to know people's names, starting with the volunteers."

Rausch sits back in his chair, folding his large hands in his lap, and there's a slight tilt to his lip. "Okay then."

He stands and I follow as we make our way around the room, while Rausch gestures for each of them to introduce themselves because he doesn't know all of them either. Angie is the only one I've met, a recent Georgetown graduate who was all too eager to take charge of the volunteers.

My smile doesn't come easily as I shake hands and thank them for volunteering. I'm missing someone. The campaign has been my savior for the past few months to keep me from thinking about her. But of course, I do still think of her, the wound not yet closed, and I don't know if it ever will.

The small bell at the top of the door jingles, a leftover from the hardware store that used to occupy this space. In walks Ethel Jackson, her crochet bag tucked under her arm. She looks around the space approvingly, her eyes finally meeting mine.

"Looks like a bunch of pomp and circumstance to me," she says, looking at me skeptically.

"Are you looking to volunteer?" I raise a challenging eyebrow.

"I thought you could use my sunny disposition."

I can't help but smile. "Well then, I have a spot for you right over here." I lead the way to an empty desk near the windows where she sets down her crochet bag, a piece of yarn making its way out of the top like it has a mind of its own.

"Is this the famous Ethel?" Rausch asks.

Ethel places a hand on her hip and looks up at him as he towers over her short, round frame. If I was a betting man, my money would be on Ethel if these two were pitted against each other. "I don't know about famous, but whatever you've heard,"—she pauses and gives him a naughty smile—"it's probably true."

Rausch laughs. Apparently, Ethel can win over anyone.

"Where's that pretty wife of yours?" she asks.

The mention of Evangeline pulls at the edges of my wound, pain ripping through me like a lightning bolt.

Before I can make an excuse, Rausch bellows over the noise. "Angie!" She makes her way over. "This is Ethel, and she would like to volunteer."

"People say I got a voice like honey, so if you want to put me on the phones, that's fine by me," Ethel proposes.

I give Rausch a thankful nod and retreat to my office. The desk is a secondhand one from the nearby school. There are strict rules on how campaign donations can be used. Right now, funds are limited as we start ramping up requests that can sometimes feel like begging. My last name can only carry me so far, and my reputation precedes me.

"Excuse me, are you Darren Walker?" A young man inquires from the doorway.

I nod and he drops an envelope on my desk. "You've been served," he says, and leaves just as quickly as he arrived.

An envelope from a law office in Arizona.

I know exactly what it is. Like a Band-Aid, I rip the envelope open to expose the wound.

Divorce papers.

Pulling off my tie, I throw it across the room. It flutters through the stagnant air and lands silently on the dirty linoleum floor.

"Don't forget about the fundraising event this weekend," Rausch says as he enters my office. He sees my tie on the ground and picks it up. When he places it on the desk he notices the papers.

"You can gloat if you want to," I tell him angrily, using him as a punching bag. "You got what you wanted, right?" I look up at him, the sting of getting the papers still fresh.

"If you want me to say that Evangeline leaving was the best thing for your campaign, then fine, but that doesn't mean I'm happy about seeing you in turmoil."

I scoff. "In turmoil? Is that what you think this is?"

"No." A look of understanding crosses his face like a shadow. "I understand your heartbreak."

I never thought of Rausch as a person, just a thorn in my side, giving me disapproving looks and lectures about getting my life together. Of course he knows what heartbreak is. No human gets a pass on that in their lifetime, not even someone as impenetrable as Rausch.

"You can think what you want, Darren, but what I said to you before was the truth. I would have done everything within my power to protect her."

I lift my eyes from the papers. "Well, it seems she didn't want to be a part of this life after all." I can't seem to keep the disappointment out of my voice.

Rausch lets out a breath. "You can sit here and stare at those papers, or you can pull yourself together and win this election."

"It's that easy, huh?"

"No. It's not easy, Darren," he sighs and resolves to take a seat. "But you can channel those emotions into something productive, because dwelling on it will do you no good." He looks through the glass partition. "Your father would have loved to see this." He smiles sadly.

"That's funny, because I would think he's shaking his head because I'm running as a Democrat," I offer a small smile.

Rausch laughs. "I don't think he would care what party you were running under. It's the fact that you're running that would matter the most to him."

"Why?" I inquire. "Why did it matter so much to him that I follow in his footsteps?"

Rausch shakes his head as if he can't believe I don't know the answer. "He didn't want you following in his footsteps. Politicians are a dime a dozen. But people who can inspire and cause real change are rare."

I shake my head. "He was the inspiring one, not me."

"Sure, he had a way of commanding a crowd," he explains. "But it didn't come naturally to him. It was something he learned—perfected, like calligraphy."

I let out a laugh, because only Rausch could use calligraphy as an example.

"But you?" He points at me, getting my attention again. "You don't even have to try. You're not following in his footsteps. You've already eclipsed him. Why do you think the press were so interested in you? They've been chomping at the bit for you to run. Not because you're Kerry Walker's son, but because you are *Darren* Walker."

Maybe he's just blowing smoke up my ass, but if I was feeling pressure before, I feel the immense weight of it now.

"Then why don't I feel like that person?"

"I can't answer that for you. I only know that your father was so hard on you because he had to work so hard for something that came so naturally to you. And you took it for granted."

"I don't know what he saw," I admit. "I was a fuckup. I would have gotten kicked out of boarding school if it weren't for his influence with the chancellor."

"Ah yes," Rausch taps his fingers against his thigh. "The great square pizza revolt," he grumbles.

"Pizza should not be square," I insist.

"Well, convincing your classmates to take over the cafeteria wasn't the way to handle it."

"My father was so pissed." I manage to laugh about it now, but back then I had real fear. I sat in the chancellor's office with the prospect of being expelled.

"And you don't think you're inspirational."

"I hardly believe that I should be proud of causing a revolt at St. Luke's," I scoff.

"Do you think it was dumb luck that you got the entire class to follow you for something reckless and stupid?"

I didn't think of it that way.

"You could have had any career you wanted in politics, but you chose to lead from my father's shadow. Why?" I ask.

"Sometimes it's better to be the kingmaker than the king," he says with a tilt to his lips.

"So, you're aware that's what people call you?" I inquire in surprise.

"I know everything, Darren."

We stare at each other in silence as I take in the weight of our conversation.

"Darren," he says, cutting through the heavy silence. "This might not be the right place to…"

"Sorry to interrupt, but the signs came in," Angie smiles excitedly, holding up a sign with my face on it and the words *Dare to elect change*, a slogan I reluctantly signed off on. "We need to know where you want the volunteers to start."

Rausch adjusts his tie and stands. "I emailed the map to Russell the other day."

"Well, he can't find it," Angie explains.

"Emails don't just disappear," he grumbles.

He follows Angie to the door but stops to look back at me. His fingers tap against the doorframe before he exits.

2

Anonymous Donor

Darren

In the bathroom mirror, I adjust my bowtie and drag in a deep breath because when I open that door, I'll be pulled into the melee of clinking champagne flutes, fake smiles, and narcissistic conversations.

Alistair disappeared shortly after the fundraiser started, leaving me on my own, and when I find him again, I'm going to wring his skinny neck.

As soon as I exit the bathroom, Penelope Van Der Walt corners me against a French nineteenth-century side table. She looks very different from the last time I saw her. More adult than kid, and I suppose that's right because when I do the math in my head, I realize that she has to be at least eighteen.

The older she gets, the more she looks like her mother Caroline with her blonde hair, green eyes, the high cheekbones of a distant aristocrat, and a petite but strong frame.

"Darren Walker," she says, a bit too excited to be running into me. All I can see is the gangly kid that kept pretending to drown in the backyard pool so that I would put my lips on hers to do CPR. After the second drowning, I got wise to her.

"Penelope, I thought you were in Switzerland." I relent, while edging away from her.

"I graduated," she reveals, playing with the lapel of my suit jacket. "And I'm home for the summer," she exhales forlornly.

"I didn't know. Congratulations!" I exclaim, honestly excited for her.

"You're not the only one who forgot." she sighs. "Apparently, my parents planned a trip for that weekend and didn't make it." She grabs a glass of champagne off the tray of a passing waiter.

"What about Alistair?"

"He has a job." She makes a face. "Can you believe it?"

"Should you be drinking?"

"Do you think anyone will notice?" She downs about half the glass in one swig.

"Okay." I grab it from her and place it on the side table. "I think that's enough."

"You can't tell me what to do in my own home," she says snottily.

"Where's your brother?" I ask through gritted teeth and look desperately through the crowd for Alistair, or anyone for that matter.

Penelope slumps against the nearby sofa. "This party's boring and not even you want to hang out with me," she glowers.

"Look," I mumble, scratching the back of my neck. "It's been a long night. I'm sorry."

"I can't believe this is all for you." She looks around the room at tuxedo-clad waiters carrying expensive champagne and delicate appetizers, weaving among beautiful floral arrangements that complement the original Brodinsky paintings.

"Didn't they do *something* to celebrate your graduation?"

"Oh, Caroline presented me with a new car, and then Remington argued that we have a driver, so why would I need one, and after that, I just tuned them out and went to my room," she bemoans.

"I'm sure they're proud of you. Alistair too," I point out.

"Darren," Bethany interrupts, giving me a peck on the cheek.

"So nice to see you."

"This is a great turnout," Bethany says, gesturing around the room.

"Caroline outdid herself," I admit. "Don't you think?" I look to include Penelope in the conversation, but she's gone.

"Well, yes, but that's not what I meant," she explains, touching my arm. "Caroline can only set the guest list but whether they actually show up is another feat entirely, and one that you seem to have accomplished." She smiles with a pride that makes her blue eyes bright.

"I'm sure it's more of wanting to see the fish in the fishbowl." I raise a teasing eyebrow.

"You can't take a compliment, just like your mother." She shakes her head.

"How is retirement treating you?" I ask, changing the subject.

"I feel like I'm busier now than when I was working, especially lately," she sighs.

"All good things I hope?"

"Very good indeed. You'd be happy to know that we're expanding Compton House." She takes a sip of her champagne.

"I wasn't aware." I haven't had time to keep up with anything that didn't involve the campaign.

"We just got the permits, and the recent donation is going to make such a huge difference," she gushes.

"Sounds like Audrina is doing her job well," I tease.

Bethany shakes her head. "You don't have to pretend with me," she winks. "I know it was you."

"I'm sorry, I don't know what you mean."

"The donation of course," she explains. "I know I shouldn't have said anything, but Darren, five million dollars is going to make such a difference."

Five million dollars.

Compton House.

It's too much of a coincidence to ignore.

"Will you excuse me?" I don't wait for an answer before weaving through the crowd, trying not to be rude.

As I make a turn down the quiet hallway, Alistair grabs my arm and hauls me up a flight of stairs. He opens the window and steps out onto the roof, waving a hand for me to follow him.

I'm not a teenager anymore. I'm a candidate for the House of Representatives. I shouldn't be climbing out of windows and escaping parties thrown to raise money for my campaign.

Against my better judgement, I climb through the window and into the night air, my dress shoes sliding on the shingles. I manage to take a seat, letting my legs hang off the edge.

"Thought you could use an escape, since hiding in the bathroom wasn't working out for you," Alistair jokes, and I smile.

"Who says I was hiding in the bathroom?" I take off my jacket and lay it on the wood shingles next to me.

Alistair gives me a look.

"Okay, I was earlier, and then I ran into your sister. She looks, um…" I'm at a loss for words. "All grown up."

"Dare, you're my best friend, but if you try anything with my sister," he pauses. "Well, she'd be punishment enough, but also, just wrong."

"What? God no." I pull at my collar, losing the bow tie.

Alistair has already discarded his suit jacket and tie, his shirt unbuttoned and laying open.

"Good, because she's a nightmare," Alistair shakes his head. "I feel sorry for her future husband."

I laugh. "She's not the only nightmare."

"Look, I don't want you to think I'm not appreciative of your parents…" I apologize.

"Don't worry. It's *a lot*. Caroline went overboard tonight. Did you happen to see the lobster crostini? She doesn't offer those unless she's pulling out the big guns." Alistair winks.

"Unfortunately, I didn't get a chance to eat anything." My stomach rumbles, but I don't have an appetite. "I'm surprised she even offered to host the fundraiser for me since I traded in my red card for blue."

"Caroline and Remington always back a winner." He pulls a flask from his pocket and hands it to me. "It's Macallan."

"What's the occasion?" I take it from him.

"To the millions of dollars being thrown at you tonight— and not because you've taken your shirt off and given them a lap dance." He chuckles and I take a swig, handing it back to him.

"I think you give my lap dance skills too much credit," I tease, but I sense a quiet shift as Alistair leans back.

The darkness shrouds much of the grounds below. Only the soft light of the party reaches across the cobblestone to the path of the gardens.

"I don't know how my father did it," I whisper.

"I'm sure it takes a special breed. I don't think I could do it," he admits.

The confidence people have in me, enough to donate hundreds of thousands of dollars, is a bit unnerving and electrifying at the same time.

"I had an interesting conversation with Bethany York tonight." I scoop up the flask and take a drink, hoping for some liquid courage.

"Did she proposition you or something?" Alistair jokes as he takes it back from me.

"She told me someone donated five million dollars to the Abigail Pershing Foundation." I turn to look at him. "Specifically, to Compton House." I raise my eyebrows.

Alistair tilts his head curiously, "It is a charity."

"Five million dollars exactly."

"Billionaires like even numbers," he reasons.

"From an anonymous donor."

"Not all billionaires want a plaque in their honor for donating to a good cause." He throws his hands in the air. "Okay, that was a stretch," he smiles.

I turn away from him. I know it was her. Who else could it have been?

He then places a hand on my shoulder. "Don't torture yourself."

"I've been torturing myself for the last three months." I stand up and steady myself on the uneven roof.

"Come on, Dare." He stands next to me. "She took the money and left. Does it matter why?"

"Of course it matters."

"I threw myself into the campaign hoping it would take my mind off her, but it hasn't, and this," I throw my arm towards the open window, to the party still going on below us, and turn back to Alistair. "Proves one thing."

I slide my leg inside the window while Alistair asks, "Proves what?"

"That she loves me." I slip inside the window.

"Where are you going?" he calls after me.

"Somewhere I should have gone all along," I answer.

I pull at the collar of my shirt. Rausch's elbow is visible on the armrest of the high-back chair in front of an unused fireplace. He's still wearing the tux he had on at the fundraiser, and he leans over to look at me as he hears me enter the study.

"Did you know?"

He pinches his brows together and then sits back in his chair, casually crossing his legs. His dress shoes sit next to the chair, so he's only in his socked feet.

"Darren, there are a lot of things I know so you might need to be more specific."

I've never been in Rausch's house before. The room is decorated in a monochromatic minimalist style—very geometrical—from the wallpaper to the Sean Scully painting hanging above the fireplace. Sitting on the side table next to him is a book.

"I'm talking about Evangeline," I fume. "Did you know she donated the money to Compton House?"

"Why do you think I know anything about that?" he challenges wearily.

"Because you know everything that goes on," I say, as if it should be obvious.

He lets out a small laugh. "That's usually true."

"You knew and you didn't want me to go after her because it would hurt the campaign," I accuse.

He shakes his head. "Do you think I'm that cruel?"

"I know exactly how you feel about her. You've made no attempt to hide it," I raise my voice, but Rausch remains stoic.

"How I feel about her is irrelevant."

"Bullshit. You've been pulling strings since the beginning. You did it with my father, and now you're doing it with me," I accuse.

"I never pulled the strings with your father."

"Don't play games. You know what she means to me," I plead.

"I know." He stands up, taking the book with him and placing it back in its slot on the bookshelf. All the spines are perfectly lined, nothing out of place, just like him.

"How do you know she donated the money?" he questions, standing in front of the bookshelf with his hands in his pockets. I've never seen Rausch look anything less than impeccable.

Tonight he looks different—vulnerable—not as impenetrable with his dress shirt unbuttoned, bow tie hanging loose and socked feet. Even his hair looks as if he's run a hand through it, the dark locks unruly and out of place.

"Bethany mentioned it. She thought I had donated it," I explain, slumping onto the leather loveseat. The anger has started to ebb away.

"If Bethany thinks you donated the money, then what makes you think Evangeline did?" He refills his glass tumbler with some clear liquid and gestures to make one for me, but I decline.

"An anonymous donation for five million dollars is not a coincidence."

He ponders something that I think should be quite obvious.

"She didn't want to hold me back." I shake my head. "She thought she was a liability."

I peer over at him in the chair where he sits casually, holding the tumbler with his thumb and forefinger precariously on the edge of the armrest.

"If you knew that's why she left, then why didn't you go after her?" he asks, taking a sip, the liquid causing his lips to glisten.

"Because she took the money," I say through gritted teeth.

He shakes his head and sets the glass on the side table.

"You don't care about the money," he rebukes as if he can read me so well and it angers me that he does.

"I didn't think she cared about the money, either," I challenge him.

"Why did you let her go?"

"I didn't *let* her go," I say, exasperated. "She left. I got out of my exam feeling like I could conquer the world and found out she took the money."

Rausch drags in a breath as if it takes effort. "Of all the ways for someone to leave…" he pauses, looking forward towards the bookshelf. "Death is the kindest."

I stand up. "I don't need Emerson quotes. I need the truth. Did you know? Did you make her leave so you could get what you wanted?" I accuse.

"Would it make it hurt any less if I said I did?" he raises his voice, standing to his full height.

I shake my head, confused.

"I wanted you to run, Darren. I wanted you to stop being a little shit and realize who you could be," he stops, running a hand over his mouth before continuing. "But I wouldn't break you in the process."

"What does that even mean?"

"I wouldn't be that cruel," he says, eyes glistening. "Because I know—I know," he stops, slumping back into the chair.

It's then that I realize he's drunk. Not the sloppy kind of drunk that makes you stand on a table and quote Emerson, but the kind that makes you sentimental.

"Maybe she donated the money, but does it even matter? You love her. You found someone who complements you, who makes you a better person, and fuck what the press thinks or what the voters think because what is the point of doing something good with your life if you don't have her by your side while you do it?" He looks just as shocked as I am when he finishes his speech.

"Rausch," I say quietly, wanting to—I don't know— because I've never seen him like this. "Why aren't you at the fundraiser?"

"You seemed to be doing fine without me." He takes another drink.

I sigh, all the air whooshing out of me like a deflating balloon. "I hid in the bathroom for a bit," I admit.

"But you found your way out." As if I had accomplished something extraordinary instead of finding the handle to the bathroom door.

"That's not what someone who wins elections does," I admit sheepishly.

"Who says?"

I open my mouth and close it.

"You're human. Evangeline's human. She just...didn't find her way out of the bathroom. Perhaps you should help her." He lifts an eyebrow. "It's been a long day," he says abruptly and places a hand on my shoulder. "I trust you can find your way out."

Then he leaves and I'm standing in his study alone, reeling. I look to the bookshelf, my eyes finding the space where one book is not perfectly lined up, the spine sticking out slightly farther than the others.

The Collected Works of Ralph Waldo Emerson.

3

Peachy Evangeline

I don't have to be at work for another hour, but I secure my apron before grabbing the book and shoving it inside. The less time I have to spend at home the better. Especially since my stepfather moved back in.

As I tread lightly through the living room, I don't see Jimmy in the recliner with the TV on. Maybe he's still asleep or better yet, maybe he never came home last night. But those daydreams are short-lived as I turn the corner into the kitchen and almost smack right into him.

"Whoa there, you in a hurry?" he asks, flashing me a smile as I back away from him. Jimmy's tall and lanky, with thinning brown hair almost the same color as his eyes and deep lines on his face from working construction. Not that he's done much of that lately.

"Some of us have to work," I quip, and when I try to move around him, he blocks me by leaning his tattooed hand on the doorframe.

I regret not buttoning my uniform all the way when his eyes dip into my shirt. But it's not so much his eyes I'm worried about when he takes hold of the string securing my apron in place. "Nice uniform."

I pull away, yanking the string from his grasp. "I'm gonna be late." I push past him and yank open the door.

"Rent is due on the first," he calls from behind me.

I turn around in shock. "Excuse me?"

"You need to be good for something around here." He taps his fingers on the doorframe before retreating into the living room.

I clench my fists, letting the door slam shut behind me. My mother's sitting on the front porch smoking a cigarette. She looks tired, like she didn't sleep, and when she hears me she looks up.

"What's Jimmy talking about?"

She throws the butt to the ground and steps on it. Mimi hated cigarette butts on the front porch, but I keep my mouth shut and focus on the real issue.

"Everyone has to pay their way around here."

I shake my head. "I helped you for years with this house. It should have been paid off by now."

She looks up at me with at least some remorse in her eyes.

"We had to take out a second mortgage when Jimmy hurt himself on the job and lost the contract for the new mini-mart," she explains.

"Yeah, well he doesn't seem to be walking with a limp now," I challenge.

"We're doing the best we can," she demands. "You think I want to lose the house?"

How stupid I was to believe anything she says.

"You know I don't have that kind of money."

"Would have been nice if you'd taken a divorce settlement from that billionaire ex-husband of yours," she complains, sticking the knife into my heart just a little bit further. "It's not like he'd have missed it."

"I told you I didn't want anything from him."

"Jesus, Evangeline. You and your pride are why we're stuck here," she accuses.

I was fooled into thinking that her tears at Mimi's funeral were genuine and that she wanted to get to know me again. I wanted to have a family so badly that I agreed to move in with her and try to rebuild our relationship, thinking our shared grief would bring us together again.

There's something in me that can't seem to let her go, even though I know it's for the best.

"What's he doing here anyway?" I wave my hand at the house with disdain.

"We needed the money."

"He's not even working," I raise my voice.

"He gets a decent disability check."

"I have a job." We could make it work without him.

"Waitressing isn't going to get us out of this hole." She waves me off.

"Well at least I'm doing something," I call over my shoulder.

I get in my car and barely give it time to warm up before I peel out of the driveway.

When I pull into the parking lot of Al's Diner, I see a shopping cart near the canal across the street, but no one under the Palo Verde tree this morning.

Eddie's already getting the griddle warmed up when I go inside, and it smells like bacon. "Your shift doesn't start for an hour." In other words, I'm not getting paid for being here early.

Ignoring him, I ask, "Have you seen Herschel?"

"You mean that homeless man you feed almost every afternoon?" he probes.

"I pay for it with my tips," I remind him sullenly.

Eddie raises an eyebrow and then shakes his head. He thinks I'm wasting my time and money on someone who should be working instead of getting a free meal.

"Didn't see him when I got here," he concedes and then goes back to prepping the kitchen.

I put my stuff away in a locker and then get started on filling ketchup bottles. When those are done, I grab the salt and pepper from inside the pantry.

Wednesday's senior discount brings in a morning rush that keeps my mind occupied and my hands busy, so that I don't even realize when it's my break time.

"How ya doin' sweetheart?" Belinda asks as I pass her by on my way to the breakroom.

"Peachy," I grumble.

"I hate to tell ya but you don't look peachy," she questions.

I hold up two one-dollar bills and she shakes her head.

"Seniors don't tip well. I told ya that," she says.

"It's like they all got together at bingo and decided that two dollars is the standard tip no matter how much the total is." I shove the bills back in my billfold.

Belinda laughs while I head into the kitchen and grab a couple pieces of bread and cheese. When I try to put it on the grill Eddie smacks my hand away with a spatula.

"Stay away from my griddle." He waves me away.

"Touchy." I laugh and hold my hands in the air as I back away.

"That's your space." He points to the dining area with the spatula. "And this is my space." He waves his hand around the kitchen.

"You're very territorial." I smile and sashay out of the kitchen while he grumbles behind me.

The whole exchange makes up for my two-dollar tips. I grab a cup of coffee and head into the breakroom. It feels like a ritual, pulling the book from my apron and opening it to my dog-eared page.

Eddie sets the grilled cheese in front of me and says, "You got a customer."

It must be Herschel, so I put the book back in my apron and pick up the grilled cheese, taking it with me.

There's only one table occupied at the back of the diner in my section. Before I reach the table, I realize it's not Herschel.

"Darren?"

4

Ex-Husband?

Darren

*S*itting outside in my rental car, I stare into the window of the diner and watch her. Her blonde ponytail sways behind her as she passes by the window every few minutes. I've been out here for nearly a half hour like a coward, unable to move, but my anger takes over, and I finally shut off the car.

When I enter the diner, I have my pick of tables. Purposefully, I choose one in her section near the back and slide into the red leather booth, tossing my sunglasses on the table. From the outside, I was expecting retro décor, and I'm not disappointed as old black and white photos hang on the light green walls. I fold my hands on the table.

The air fills with the scent of cherry blossoms and I know she's close. I tilt my head just enough to see her as she takes a step forward with a plate of grilled cheese that I didn't order.

Shock is written all over her face. "Darren?"

I rest my arm casually over the bench seat and school my face because seeing her affects me more than I was prepared for.

"What are you doing here?"

"I could ask you the same thing. Shouldn't you be relaxing on a beach somewhere instead of working in a shitty diner?" I challenge. "Since you have five million dollars and all."

She's scared.

She's scared because she knows I'll force her to admit what she doesn't want me to know.

"Yeah, well some of us prefer to be humble," she lies, and even though I'm angry and hurt I still want to kiss the truth out of her until there is nothing left to tell.

I sniff. "Humble, is that what you call it?"

"I like working." She shifts on her feet. "Unlike some people."

I look around the diner's scuffed linoleum flooring, chipped laminate tables, and ripped vinyl seats. She doesn't belong here.

She belongs with me. "Aren't you tired of pretending?"

The bell above the door chimes as a few customers enter. A red-haired waitress grabs a couple menus and directs them to a table on the other side of the diner, but her eyes curiously watch us.

"What do you want from me?" she asks with a tired voice, and I can see it in her eyes too. Like the light is starting to dim and this fucking place is what's extinguishing it.

"I want you to tell me the truth, for once," I grit out.

"Darren, I have to work." She walks away and I scramble out of the booth to follow her.

"You don't get to walk away from me—again," I scold, and my gruff voice gets the full attention of the diner.

Evangeline clenches her fists as she stands with her back to me.

"This your ex-husband?" the red-haired waitress asks.

"Ex-husband?" I bark out a laugh. "No, we're still married. I have no intention of signing those papers."

And that's when Evangeline turns around to face me, a pleading look in her eyes.

"I might look sweet, but I got mace in my apron, and I know how to use it," the waitress says, and I'm glad there's at least one person here who cares about her even a fraction as much as I do.

"It's fine, Belinda." Evangeline holds up her hand to warn her off.

Belinda hesitates, narrowing her eyes at me before she goes back to her table.

"Do they know you're a millionaire?"

"I'm taking a break," Evangeline says.

"You just had one," the cook says, poking his head out from the pick-up window.

"I'm taking another one," Evangeline calls back to him.

As we exit into the alley, she whirls around, the fiery look back in her eyes. "What do you want, Darren?"

"I want to know why you're working as a waitress when you have five million dollars."

She narrows her eyes at me. "Oh, stop it, Darren. You know I don't have the money, that's why you're here." She throws her hand up at me.

"I want to know why."

She stays silent, her lips pressed into a thin line. I have no intention of making things easy on her. Not after how she left.

"Do you know what it was like to get out of the exam and find you gone?"

There's remorse in her eyes. "Stop it."

"That was a huge day for me," I say. "You know what taking the exam meant to me."

Frustrated, I clamp the back of my neck and stare at the concrete before I finally look at her again. "If I'm being honest, because let's face it, one of us has to be, I hated you for like a second."

A shadow passes over her eyes. "You *should* hate me," she admits.

"Fuck, Evan. I told you I loved you."

"Darren," she says my name and I feel it right down to my core.

"I meant it. Every single word and you fucking left."

She turns away, wrapping her arms around her body, as if she can't bear to look at me.

"Stop running away." I take a few steps forward, but I don't touch her, not yet.

"I just saved us a goodbye that was inevitable."

"Bullshit! You ran away like a coward," I argue.

She throws her arms in the air. "This was never going to work!"

"You didn't even give us a chance."

"Because I know how it ends and it's not good for either of us," she says.

"I *know* how this ends, Evan. I've seen it. It's you and me, fucking old, surrounded by our grandchildren. *That's* how this ends," I demand, "Not here in a *fucking* alley behind a shitty diner." I can see the tears swimming in her blue eyes like the churning ocean.

She tries to move away but I back her against the building. "Admit that you love me, Evan," I demand.

She shakes her head, her blonde ponytail swaying.

"If you didn't, you wouldn't have donated the money."

My eyes drop to her lips.

Lips I've kissed countless times.

Lips that have soothed and scolded and scorched me.

Each breath is done with effort, her chest rising and falling. She looks as though she might either kiss me or knee me in the balls. I'll take whichever she's willing to give right now.

"I only wanted it to take care of my grandmother, and

she's gone," she says, her voice quiet and reserved. "It doesn't mean I love you."

I lean in, my lips so close to hers that I can feel her breath against mine. I can almost feel her heart thumping. I reach into her apron, pulling out the book. Her eyes widen and she tries to take it from me, but I pull it out of her grasp.

"You're a very bad liar, Queenie." I take a step back and hold the book before her, *A Moveable Feast*. The spine is cracked, the pages pulling away and the corners tell of once being dog-eared. Well-read and well-loved, the way a book should be.

I let her snatch the book from me and she tucks it back in her apron for safe keeping.

"It doesn't matter."

"It matters to me!" I raise my voice in frustration. Jesus she's stubborn.

"I don't belong there. Don't you see that?"

"I don't."

"Then you have blinders. You want to run for office, and I will *kill* that dream for you." She touches her chest.

"I only had that dream because of you. Do you think any of it matters when you're not there with me?" I demand. "I don't need *saving*, Evan." I take a step towards her again. "Not anymore." I brush my palm against her cheek.

She angles her head to lean against my palm as her eyes flutter.

"I want you." I run my thumb over her bottom lip as she parts them. I want nothing more than to push her over the edge until she gives in. "Why do you have to be so stubborn?" I argue, removing my hand.

"Because you and I were a bad idea from the start. I have a past that you cannot recover from."

"It's the fifth congressional district of Virginia, not President of the *goddamn* United States!" I raise my voice again.

"This is just the tip of the iceberg. I won't be the reason you don't become what you were always meant to be."

"I would have been content to squander my potential for the rest of my life," I say. "Until you. Because of you, I want it all. I want what could be. And whether I get elected or not is irrelevant. You said not trying is the real crime. Well, I'm trying. Is that not good enough?" I protest. "Am I. Not. Good. Enough?" I enunciate every word.

She hugs herself as if to keep vital organs from spilling out all over the hot pavement.

"Just sign the papers," she says. "Sign them and let me go."

"You don't want to admit that you love me, Evan, fine, but explain this to me," I insist. "Why the fuck would you go back to living in that house?"

"I didn't have a choice!" she yells.

"Well, now you do." I give her a cunning smile.

5

Burn it Down
Evangeline

*B*efore I even set foot inside, I know they're gone, but it's still a punch to the gut. The house has been stripped bare.

All the furniture in the living room is gone. I run down the hallway to my mother's bedroom and find her closet empty and indents in the carpet where her bed used to be. Even the pictures that hung on the wall are gone.

I'm still wearing my apron as I stand in the middle of the living room, the corner of the book jabbing at my upper thigh.

I see his shadow before he steps around the corner.

"What did you do?"

Darren steps into the light, taking in the empty room with its dusty curtains and worn wallpaper as if he had nothing to do with it.

"It always amazes me what some people will give up for money," he says, eyes trained on me, hands in his pockets as if he's on a casual walk instead of turning my life upside down—yet again.

"How much?" I demand while clenching my fists.

Darren tilts his head, a few pieces of dark hair falling over his forehead.

"How much did you pay them to leave?"

There's a flicker of remorse in his expression. "Does it matter?" he asks.

"It matters." I want to know how much I was worth to them.

"I bought the house for market value, and I paid them an additional sum to be out by the end of the day." He looks around at the empty house. "I'm impressed they followed through with it."

My legs start to give out and I have to place my hands on my thighs to steady myself. I let out a small, painful laugh.

"I guess you learned not to overpay people."

"I would have paid them anything they wanted just to get her and that piece of shit stepfather of yours out of your life," he admits. "That's what they asked for, so that's what I gave them."

My knees buckle and Darren reaches out to steady me, but I bat him away.

"Are you so angry I left that you'd offer them money just to prove a point?"

"I didn't do it to prove a point," he reassures.

"You can't help fucking with my life!" I yell at him.

"I wouldn't have to if you had just taken the money and gotten the hell away from them," he explains. "At least I could have dealt with that, but not this." He motions around the house in disgust and it's that look in his eyes that I can't bear.

I know what he sees.

"What happened to you?" he shakes his head.

I look at him in confusion.

"When I first met you, I was sleeping with one eye open, afraid you'd try to smother me in my sleep," he jokes darkly.

"Then I find you living back here with these people," he says with disdain.

"She was the only family I had left!" I yell, my voice echoing through the empty room and off the walls.

He raises his voice. "And you are *my* family!" He taps his chest. "You had five million dollars. You could have gone anywhere. You could have had any life. Instead, you donated it all and came back here to work as a waitress, living with your stepfather," he accuses. "You cannot ask me to have that knowledge and be fine with it," he continues.

"I couldn't keep your money."

"I know," he says quietly. "Because you love me."

"I don't love you, Darren," I grit out.

He smiles with that wolfish grin like he knows a secret. "If you say so. You want to deny that you love me, fine. You don't want to come back to Washington with me? Fine." He pulls a lighter from his pocket. Flicking it on, he watches the bright red flame dances in the drafty room. "But in no world would I ever accept you living here with them," he raises his voice.

"So you can hate me all you want, but I'll sleep well knowing they're far away from you," he grits out, snapping the lighter closed.

He takes a step forward, grabbing my hand roughly and placing the lighter in my palm. "The house is yours, Evangeline. I bought it for you. Burn it down if that's what you want."

6

Rearview Mirror

Evangeline

I can hear the coyotes from inside the house. They're loud tonight, but that's not what's keeping me awake. It's not just the emptiness of this house, but that it's devoid of anything that reminds me of home. There's nothing left but bad memories.

I break down and do something I swore I wouldn't. I pick up the phone and dial Cleo. She answers on the first ring.

"What's wrong?" she asks.

"What makes you think something's wrong?"

She makes a tsk noise. "For one, it's past midnight, and two, you never call me. You always text me some bullshit emoji as proof of life," she quips.

I didn't even realize it was that late. "I'm sorry, did I wake you?"

"Have you met me?" she jokes.

I manage to let out a laugh.

"I miss you," I sniffle.

"I miss you too."

"It's just been a rough couple of days. Nothing I can't handle," I lie. "I just wanted to hear your voice."

"Do you want to tell me about it?" she probes.

"No," I sigh.

I grip the phone tighter, hearing her voice making me emotional.

"Will you tell me about your day?" I ask and pull the covers up and over my head as I cradle the phone between my ear and the pillow.

"Well, you're not gonna believe this…"

Something tickles my nose and I swat it away. The heaviness of sleep starts to lift. I was on the phone with Cleo, but I must have fallen asleep. I swipe my hand along the sheets, searching for my phone, when I bump into what feels like an arm.

An arm that's attached to a body.

I whip the blanket back to reveal Cleo staring back at me with her golden-brown eyes and dark curly hair pressed to the pillow next to me.

"Did you drive all night?" I ask her.

"Don't worry, your snoring kept me awake on the drive down." She smiles while handing me my missing phone.

I snatch it from her and laugh. "I do not snore."

"Whatever you say, honey." She looks at me thoughtfully.

"I don't," I protest further as I settle back onto the pillow, the shock of her being here wearing off.

"You really didn't have to come."

"You don't want me here?" she quips.

"That's not what I meant. I just didn't want you coming all the way down here for nothing," I explain.

She props her head up with her hand, resting her elbow on the pillow and giving me a no bullshit kinda look.

"Have you been out of this bed lately?" she inquires.

I scowl. "What do you mean?" I'm sure my breath smells

because I fell asleep without brushing, and maybe I could use a shower, but I can't be that bad.

"Well, either you got robbed in the middle of the night or something else is going on that you most certainly *weren't* gonna tell me about." She narrows her eyes at me and I flip over on my back, blocking out the sun with my forearm.

"I need coffee." I sit up and she makes a disgruntled noise. Turning to look at her, I roll my eyes. "I'll tell you everything over a cup of coffee."

She concedes, and we make our way into the kitchen. I start the coffee maker—that I had to buy to replace the one my mother took—and grab two Styrofoam cups that I stole from work. While the coffee's brewing, Cleo inspects the Splenda packets and the creamers I also absconded from the diner

"Are you gonna tell me what happened?" She looks around the empty kitchen and living room.

It feels like we're just two girls from the desert as we sit with our bare feet propped up wearing cut-off shorts and tank tops on the back patio. It's early enough in the day and the clouds are keeping the heat at bay, at least for now.

She leans over and tucks a stray piece of hair behind my ear. "Oh honey, you were meant for so much more."

I shake my head. "Mimi used to say that if you keep looking in the rearview mirror you'll never see what's right in front of you."

"Smart lady. Too bad you didn't listen to her."

"Excuse me?"

"You heard me. If what you told me in the kitchen earlier was true, then I don't know why you're still here."

I look at her in shock. "Now you're on Darren's side?"

"I'm not on anyone's side."

"You think it's okay for him to just come in here and…"

"Save you from yourself?" she challenges.

Cleo follows me back inside the house. "I don't need saving." I glower.

"Look around you," Cleo says. "*What* are you doing here?"

"I'll fix it up when I have the money." I dump the rest of my coffee in the sink angrily.

"I'm talking about you being back here in the first place."

"You know I came back for Mimi's funeral," I argue.

"Why did you stay?" she asks.

I grab the edge of the counter because her question knocks the air out of me. I've lied to myself too many times and it's catching up to me.

"I needed her to love me," I admit, and it feels like the ground is opening up and about to swallow me whole. When I look at Cleo, her brown eyes glisten with sympathy. "Why didn't she love me?"

Cleo's arms are instantly around me and I hold onto her.

"It's not your fault," she soothes.

"I know," I confirm and wipe my eyes. "But why does it feel like there's something inside me that's not good enough to be loved."

Cleo leans against the counter. "It's like I said, you're too busy looking in the rearview mirror that you don't see what's right in front of you."

"You don't understand."

"No, I don't understand how you can walk away from a man who genuinely loves you."

"I think… I think it's too late."

"If I'm right, that man would wait until the end of days for you," she smiles, taking my chin in her hand. "But you gotta go back to find out."

7

What Took You So Long?

Darren

"I'm fielding questions about your marital status." Rausch slides his phone back into his pocket while we walk towards the park.

"Don't the press have better things to do?"

"You've been campaigning for three months, and your wife is nowhere to be found."

"Can we talk about this later?" I go through my notes, avoiding the conflict, when normally I fall headfirst into it.

"Well, I need to know what to say," he counters. "*You* need to know what to say."

"I don't know, because I wasn't planning on having to tell them anything," I raise my voice.

I was planning that she would be here.

"This is important. You need to be on top of your game. The press will be there," Rausch persists.

"I know," I snap and then let out a breath. "I'm waiting."

Rausch turns to look at me with a curious gaze.

"Explain to me why we're doing this again?" I ask.

"You need to get your face out there," he replies.

"My face is on every street corner," I counter.

"And now we need to get your face on TV."

"'Scuse me?" I whip my head in his direction.

"You have a face for TV," Rausch compliments.

"Well, yeah, but," I stop. "Don't distract me from the real issue here."

He stops walking and lets out a breath. "I know this is not what you want to hear, but it's my job…"

"It's your job to tell me the ugly truth," I interrupt. "But can we put the ugly on hold for today?"

Rausch concedes by giving me a disgruntled nod.

I pull at my collar, the warm spring air already causing me to sweat.

"I hate suits," I grumble.

"Stick to the speech," Rausch retorts, getting back to business. "Talk about the union, bringing more business to the area…" He continues, but I've already tuned him out. I look at the small crowd that has gathered and groan internally.

"The ones with Walker signs—did you pay them to be here?" I accuse.

Rausch stays silent.

I narrow my eyes at him.

"Gently persuaded," he offers. "But look," he points to a few attendees with Calhoun signs. "They came on their own."

"Great turnout!" Angie beams, looking at the small crowd, and she's either blind or being paid by Rausch to blow smoke up my ass. She doesn't wait for my reply and starts getting the microphone ready.

I walk through the crowd and introduce myself while I wait for Angie to get everything set up, and see Ethel waving me over to a group of seniors.

"I don't usually leave my house," a white-haired lady says. "And I certainly don't get involved in politics, but I don't want to lose my house," she says. "Ethel said if I voted for you, that wouldn't happen."

I look to Ethel, who clutches her crochet bag tight to her chest. She offers me a small smile.

"Well, I can't make any promises," I start to say.

"Isn't that what politicians do, make promises?"

"Most of them, yeah, but if you're facing the same issue Ethel was, the only way we can combat that is to introduce the bill for the property tax relief program again," I explain.

"You can do that?" she questions, and I can see the hopefulness in her eyes, as if it's already a done deal.

"If I'm elected, I can reintroduce it, but I can't guarantee it will pass. It has to be voted on by the other representatives," I explain.

"Darren, we're ready," Angie pronounces, touching my arm to get my attention.

I hold a hand up for her to wait. "I just want to do what's right for the community." I look between Ethel and her friends.

I walk with Angie up to the podium. "You're very sweet," Angie says, handing me the microphone.

I let out a small laugh. "Not sure I've ever been called sweet before."

"You really care about these people. It's the reason I wanted to work on the campaign. This is like a dream come true for me," she gushes.

"Thanks," I say as she adjusts my tie.

"I'll see you back at the campaign office?"

"You're not staying?"

"I'll be back with some of the volunteers to take everything down, but Rausch asked me to go pick up the pins from the printer. Insisted, really," she rolls her eyes with a laugh.

"Hmm." I press my lips together, looking over at Rausch as he greets one of the police officers that was hired for crowd control. An expense we overestimated considering the small number of people in attendance.

Standing at the podium, the sun beats down on me and I

can feel beads of sweat down the back of my neck. Rausch stands to the side, giving me an encouraging gesture to get on with it. I have my speech in my hand.

I can't help feeling how different I am than them. Wearing this expensive suit, sweating in the sun while they look eagerly on, waiting for me to change their lives. I take my jacket off and throw it over the podium.

The crowd shuffles their feet, and Rausch gives me a nervous look.

"I never intended to run to be your representative. I didn't think I was cut out for politics. I would have happily lived off my trust fund, but then I had the fortunate opportunity to meet one of the community's residents." I smile at Ethel, who's fanning herself with a pamphlet. "She was ready to beat me with her cane because she thought I was an investor, ready to scoop up another house in the neighborhood and turn it into a McMansion, as she so eloquently called it." I loosen my tie, leaving it hanging precariously against my dress shirt. The crowd chuckles a little bit.

"It's called cleaning up the neighborhood. Attracting people to live here!" Someone with a Calhoun sign calls from the back.

There are a few rumbles from the crowd. "Revitalization of older neighborhoods can be a good thing." I hear a few protests. "But not at the expense of the most vulnerable of residents who live on fixed incomes.

"I have to admit, I was angry. Angry enough to try and think of ways to help her. But change, real change, comes from being involved with the very policies that impact the community. I want to be that change."

The crowd cheers and then someone asks, "That's big talk, but how are you gonna do that? I've got abandoned shops on either side of me on Main Street. That ain't a good look." The man furrows his brow while crossing his arms over his chest. "We need people to invest in the community."

"I can't make promises that I'll be able to make everyone happy because that's simply not feasible," I explain. "But I *can* promise that I will listen because that's what being your representative means. I'm your voice in one of the most influential areas of our government."

I flip through my notecards. "So let me help you understand where I stand on some important issues." I continue through my speech, making adjustments as needed. "If you'll let me, I'd like to be that voice of change for you in Congress," I finish.

Up front, Ethel claps vigorously and people raise their signs.

Some reporters from the local newspapers push to the front, hands raised, press passes swinging around their necks.

"Mr. Walker?" an older gentleman grabs my attention, and I nod for him to continue. "You're running as a Democrat, but your father was a Republican representing the state of Virginia, do you think that will influence your party ties?"

"I don't like party ties. I never have. I think we should vote for what is right and what is best for the community, not because it's in line with how our party votes."

"Don't you think that will make you unpopular in the House?" another reporter asks.

I laugh. "Probably." I shrug.

"Your father promised to shake things up in Congress, but you could argue his record shows otherwise," someone else comments.

"I can't tell you why my father voted the way he did on certain issues, and well, he's not here for you to question," I note sadly, causing a few of them to shuffle on their feet. "I can only tell what *I* will do."

"Where's your wife? We haven't seen her with you at any of the rallies," someone questions.

Rausch steps forward to put a stop to the personal questions, but I hold my hand up.

"Her grandmother passed, and she's been handling things back home," I explain, and Rausch presses his lips together disapprovingly.

When I look at the crowd, I can't school the shock and elation on my face as I notice Evangeline standing at the back.

"Excuse me," I say into the mic. "I haven't seen my wife in a while."

I jump down from the stage and push my way through the crowd until I reach her. Gathering her into my arms, I don't hesitate to crash my mouth to hers, tasting salty tears. She kisses me back, her arms wrapping around my shoulders and her fingers splayed in my hair.

Everything fades into the background until it's just her and me, the way it should be.

Holding her face in mine, I rest my forehead against hers while I wipe a stray tear from her cheek. I breathe her in, the sweet scent of cherry blossoms.

"What took you so long?"

8

A Politician, Not A Rockstar

Evangeline

"I think you like to make my life harder," Rausch complains as we walk through the crowd.

"An unintentional benefit." Darren flashes me a wolfish grin, causing my stomach to flip.

Ethel approaches and I look at her campaign lanyard with surprise. It feels like there's so much I missed.

"I'm part of crowd control." She looks at the few people that are left lingering in the park.

I laugh. "It's good to see you."

She looks me up and down critically and then nods. "It's good to see you too," she says as if there's a double meaning in there.

"Stop monopolizing my wife," Darren interrupts.

Ethel pulls her bag further up on her shoulder. "I don't get paid enough to put up with your attitude," she teases.

"You're a volunteer. You don't get paid," Darren says.

Ethel's mouth drops open. "We need to revisit this," she calls after him as we walk towards the waiting car.

"Sometimes going off the cuff has benefits," Darren revisits the conversation with Rausch.

"As if going off script is the least of our worries," Rausch retorts.

"I'm not apologizing for greeting my wife," Darren quips back.

Bailey opens the car door and Darren touches the small of my back to guide me inside. It's such a simple gesture, but it has me reeling. The spark of his fingers trails along my back as I slide into the sedan.

Rausch takes the seat opposite us, resting his hands on his thighs.

"I'm not talking about your little stage dive, although it would be good for you to remember you're a politician not a rockstar." Rausch looks at me for the first time and I can see trepidation in his eyes. I don't blame him for being wary of me.

"Aren't they one and the same?"

"Now's not the time to be funny. I'm talking about giving the press more information than they need."

My head spins as I look at Darren, and his face falls.

"It's like putting a bloodhound onto a scent. You just gave them a bone with Evangeline's name on it," he continues.

"Because I said she was settling things back home instead of campaigning with me?" he questions. "If you haven't noticed, it's not exactly a huge crowd."

"They're not going to find anything," I speak up and Rausch's gaze lands on mine.

"I think you underestimate the press," he says coolly while the back of Darren's hand brushes against my thigh as the car takes a turn.

That one touch is like an electric current that spreads outward.

"You mean the Lynchburg Bugle?" Darren jokes with a laugh.

Rausch clears his throat.

"Ellen was very good at concealing her business," I add.

"I'm sure she was, but there are other factors."

"Do we have to do this now?" Darren glances at me as I squirm in my seat.

"Sorry to break up this happy reunion," Rausch says sarcastically, "but reality is looming. What about your family?"

Darren has a sheepish grin on his face. "Taken care of."

"What is the nature of your relationship with your family?" Rausch asks me.

"Darren, it's fine," I reassure, using it as an excuse to place my hand on the top of his thigh and feel it stiffen under my palm.

"If you're such a great chess player, then wouldn't you already know?"

"Your mother, Maxine, is forty-eight years old. She was married to Lieutenant Patrick Bowen of the US Navy until his death during a training exercise…"

"Enough!" Darren raises his voice and I remove my hand. He angles his head slightly towards me.

"I know facts, not emotions." Rausch grabs the handle of the door before Bailey can pull it open.

"That's obvious." I exit the car behind them, but then I'm distracted by the campaign headquarters.

There's an unmistakable sense of pride on his face when he takes my hand and leads me inside.

"Oh good. I didn't think you were coming back," a short woman with brown hair pulled into a ponytail and cat-eye glasses grabs his attention. She's young, maybe my age, and when she puts her hand on Darren's arm in a familiar way, I feel the faint tinge of jealousy.

"I got a call from the Danville Daily, and they want to fact check a few things," she continues.

"Yeah, just give me a minute." Darren smiles at her, and I stand awkwardly until he grabs my hand.

"Angie, this is my wife, Evangeline," he introduces us, and Angie can't conceal her surprise.

"Oh," she says. "Oh, oh my god, so nice to meet you!" she exclaims a little too excitedly.

"Angie manages"—Darren pauses—"well, she manages just about everything," he laughs.

"Nice to meet you." I shake her hand.

"So, about the Danville Daily?" Angie looks at him expectantly.

"My office is right through there. I'll just be a minute," Darren offers, gesturing to the small space at the back.

His fingers linger in mine until the last minute, and Angie pulls him in the direction of one of the desks. I pass by a large poster with Darren's face on it, above the words *Dare for Change*. Him running for office in theory was so much different than the reality I find myself in.

When I enter the office, Rausch is sitting in a chair that looks too small for his large frame. He notices me and puts his phone away.

"I know you don't like me." I get straight to the point.

"Whether I like you or not is irrelevant."

"I don't know what Darren told you, but I left because—"

"I know why you left," he barks.

"And you think I should have stayed gone." I lean against the desk and cross my arms over my chest, readying for a fight.

"No," he surprises me by saying. "Do you think I liked seeing Darren heartbroken?"

When I left, *Rausch* was here picking up the pieces. I clasp my hands in front of me. "I thought I was doing the right thing."

"Darren's head hasn't been in the game, and I don't think

his heart has been in it either… not like it should be," Rausch confesses.

The small office feels even smaller with the weight of Rausch's attention on me, but I didn't come back to be pushed around by him.

"I understand that you need to know about my family situation in order to control the narrative. It might just be facts to you, but it's *personal* to me," I warn him.

Rausch nods, and silence falls like a curtain between us. I smooth down my skirt and let out a breath.

"You don't intimidate me."

"I'm glad we've gotten that out of the way." He tilts his head as if waiting for me to continue.

"I only have Darren's best interests at heart." I pause, looking down at my shoes and then back up at him.

"That is something we have in common, as difficult as that might be to accept," Rausch states with a hint of amusement.

"As long as that's the only thing," I smile.

"Well, you were right." Darren storms into the office, interrupting us.

Rausch laughs. "And this is news?"

Darren drops a paper on the desk, shaking his head, and Rausch peers over at it with a raised eyebrow.

"They made Rory look like a fucking saint!" Darren roars. "Did you know they were going to run this?"

Rausch snatches the paper but not before I see the headline. *Rory Colton's first thirty days in the late Senator Kerry Walker's congressional seat.*

"You don't need to be concerned with Rory Colton." Rausch drops the paper back on the desk and Darren takes a seat. "Jordie Calhoun is who you should be worried about." He leans back, crossing his legs and rubbing his chin. His eyes look dark and determined, and when they're trained on me, I feel a shiver travel down my spine.

Darren sighs. "Just warn me next time."

He rolls up his sleeves and I swallow hard.

"Is something wrong, Evangeline?" Darren asks with a smirk as he grips the edges of his armrest.

"No," I say quickly. "I'm just... is it hot in here?" I look around for the A/C vents.

Rausch clears his throat and then stands. "It's been a long day. I need to get home and feed my cat."

"You have a cat?" Darren asks in shock.

"Does that surprise you?" There's amusement in his eyes.

Darren shrugs. "I just didn't see you as a cat person."

"I'm not a monster, Darren. I like animals. They're surprisingly good company," he says. "Superior to most humans."

He stands by the doorway. "In fact, I think there are a lot of neglected pets around here.

"Angie!" Rausch bellows, and she appears next to him. "You have a little terrier, don't you?"

"Benson," she answers with a confused expression.

"Why don't you go home and take him for a walk? And tell the rest of the staff to go home as well." He looks back at me before he leaves, shutting the door behind him.

Darren shifts in the chair, his hazel eyes trained on me, and I shiver. "Come here," he commands in a low, rough voice.

9

Eyes On Me, Queenie

Darren

*S*he rounds the desk, nervously peering through the glass into the heart of the campaign office. I grab onto her hips, sliding her in front of me, and she lets out a startled breath. She grips the edge of the desk while I explore her thigh with my fingertip.

"Did you wear this skirt for me?" I play with the edge of the material and feel her thigh tense.

"Yes," she answers, her voice breathy.

I push her thighs apart. My hand glides under her skirt, and I find she's wearing a lace garter belt. My stomach tightens. I suppress a groan, stretching the lace, and then look up at her.

"Is this for me, too?" I inquire.

Her lips part as she nods. I let out a labored breath as I brush a finger over her panties.

She nervously looks out into the office again.

"Eyes on me, Queenie."

She snaps her head forward.

I hum as I play with the edges of her panties. "Has it been

so long that you've lost your edge?" I ask, my eyes flicking to the office where the volunteers gather their things. There are still a few stubborn laggers reluctant to leave. I like their diligence when it comes to the campaign, but right now, I want them to leave so I can flip her over, press her cheek to the cheap laminate wood of this secondhand desk, run my hand over the plump softness of her ass, and sink into her.

"No," she says. "It's just—I've missed you." She reaches for me, but I give her a look that causes her to retract her hand.

I wanted her to come back, and now that she has, I want to make her suffer for leaving me in the most delicious and tantalizing way. I want to punish her, the way that she punished me with her absence, but in the same breath I want to treasure her, worship her, drop to my knees and sink my tongue into her wet cunt so I can hear the way she moans when I make her come.

"Let's see just how *much* you missed me." I slide a finger under her panties and feel the slickness of her need. I nearly come in my pants when she shudders, her tight cunt gripping me while I slide a finger inside.

And then there's her moan, an F sharp that rings through my office. Her thighs shake and her eyes flutter.

The door bangs open, and Evangeline stiffens as Angie's head pokes inside.

"Hey, Dare, I wanted to go over the copy for the ad," she proposes.

"Angela," I say calmly while staring at my wife. "Go walk your dog."

"Sorry?" she questions with a confused expression, none the wiser that my wife is about to come.

I flick my gaze to her. "Walk. Your. Dog," I grit out, uncharacteristically. "And lock up on your way out."

Angie looks embarrassed and shuts the door behind

herself. I watch as she grabs her bag from her desk and herds a few stragglers out the door with her.

Evangeline is on the verge of falling apart. It's beautiful—she's beautiful—and I've missed her.

"Darren," she mouths breathlessly, arching her back. Her breasts rise and fall in short bursts.

Instead of making her come, I flip her over—her body resting on the desk with her perfect ass in black lacy panties on display, and I lick my lips at the sight of her. I push her skirt higher.

Hurriedly, I unbuckle my belt, pulling the leather through the loops and holding it folded in my hands. I have never been into punishment, gotten off on spanking porn, but for a moment, with the milky white of her cheeks exposed to me, wicked thoughts travel through my mind. I drop the belt, and when it hits the floor with a clank, she jumps.

I don't take her panties off but push them aside and sink into her.

Instant gratification was my old friend but I'm different now. I know how much sweeter it is to deny myself to the point of going mad because when you finally get the prize, it's so much more intense.

I've waited three months—haven't *fucked* in three months, and as torturous as it is, I move slow—deliberate—thrusting into her like a languorous kiss. Her cheek pressed to the wood, her eyes closed, an expression on her face that is both pain and pleasure, she wiggles and pushes against me, eagerly wanting more.

I oblige by reaching around and pressing a finger to her clit, making her moan louder, and I grab her hair, unable to resist any longer. I was never very good at resisting her.

It only takes a few hard, punishing thrusts, and I am gone to her—completely gone. She's my home, my family, and I'm never letting her leave me again.

10

Break Me
Evangeline

J place the Chinese take-out container on the ground with the others. They're scattered around us as we sit with our backs pressed against the wall of the office. Darren's shirt is loosely buttoned on me, and the sleeves are long and hang over my hands, but it smells like him, and I've missed that so much.

"So, this is what adulting looks like?" I tease.

"Well, not this in particular." He motions to the mess we've made of his office.

I look around, and even in the darkness with only a small lamp to illuminate the room, I admire the posters on the wall, a few pictures—one in particular—of his father during his own campaign. It looks like a gift because of the ornate frame.

"If only he could see you now," I offer.

Darren tracks my gaze to the photo. "Rausch gave that to me."

I turn to look at him. "The two of you are getting along. Seems like I missed more than I thought."

"A temporary truce, I suppose," he smiles.

"It's a good thing. He's always cared for you, and he'll make sure you win."

"What were the two of you talking about earlier when I interrupted?"

I didn't think he'd noticed. Especially since he was in uproar over Rory Colton getting front page coverage.

"A temporary truce of our own," I answer cryptically.

Darren settles back against the wall, his long legs stretched out before him.

"And Ethel?" I laugh.

"What? You don't think I can charm old ladies with canes?" he teases.

"I think if you can win her over, you can win over just about anyone," I tease back.

"I'll have you know campaigning is more than just kissing babies and shaking hands," he jests.

"What has it been like for you?" I ask in a serious tone.

"More difficult than I thought," he sighs. "You saw the rally today. I could barely get a few hundred voters to show up. And then Rory gets front page coverage, and I don't know," he lets out a frustrated breath.

"Did you think you could win on name alone?" I question.

He rests his head on the wall and angles it so he can look me in the eyes. "Maybe," he replies and then looks down at the container in his hand, pushing the food around with the chopsticks. "Everything's always come so easy. This," he motions around the office, "is out of my grasp."

"It may feel like that now, but the race isn't over yet. You still have time to turn things around." I offer him a small smile, but I can't help but feel that I will still hold him back.

Darren rests the container against his thigh. His hair is tousled, and he's bare chested, since I've appropriated with his shirt. His pants are still unbuttoned, the zipper yawning open just enough to see the smattering of dark hairs that dip below the waistband.

I wonder if I will ever get enough of him. He's already fucked me on his desk, in the chair, against the glass partition —which was flimsy enough to almost be taken down—and yet I still want him.

He sees the way I'm looking at him and smiles. Setting the container down with the others, he drags me onto his lap. Fingering the collar of his shirt that I'm wearing, he says, "You know how much I like it when you wear my shirts."

I feel the guilt bloom inside me as I remember folding his Georgetown shirt and leaving it on the bed when I left. I couldn't bear to take it with me. I yearned for it every night when I went to sleep.

I touch his face. "I'm sorry," I whisper, but in the silence of the office with the moonlight streaking in through the front blinds, it sounds louder than I meant for it to be.

He furrows his brow as he grips my waist. I feel the pads of his thumbs run along my hip bone.

"I thought I was doing the right thing," I try to explain.

"I'm stronger than you think. If you had just trusted me…" He leaves the sentence hanging.

"I trust *us*, Darren. What I don't trust is everyone else. They'll use me to get to you and I wanted to protect you from that. Protect you from *me*." I place my hand on his face, and I feel the tic in his jaw.

I know he's still angry with me. He fucked me like he didn't know if he wanted to break me or piece me back together.

"I'm back because I love you." I search his face, looking for any sign of his love in return.

"I know," he says, touching my face, and I place my palm over his, leaning into his hand like a cat searching for affection.

I feel the wedding band on his finger as it scrapes along my cheek. I run my thumb over it before threading my fingers through his.

"I couldn't take it off. I didn't choose to fall in love with you, but now that I have, I wouldn't change it. I *can't* change it, so don't ask me to."

11

Thrift Shopping
Evangeline

$\mathcal{D}$ arren kisses the tip of my nose and my eyes flutter open. The sun is horrific and I turn over, stuffing my face into the pillow. We didn't get home until late, and it's much too early to be woken up.

"I have to leave," Darren says, and I reach for him.

"No," I pull him back down. The weight of his body presses me into the mattress as I kiss him.

"I'm going to be late if you keep doing that," he smiles against my lips.

"That's the point," I laugh.

Darren props himself up on the bed and looks at me. "You make it very hard, but I have a commitment. My staff is waiting."

"You have staff?" I giggle. "That's very adult." I pull at his tie.

"Yes, you met one of them yesterday. Angie." He manages to get out of my grasp, his tie fluttering through my fingertips as he makes his way off the bed.

I roll over and watch as he readjusts it in the mirror, thinking about how handsome he looks.

"She's been a workhorse on the campaign. She organizes the volunteers and because of her background in journalism, she handles some of the media," he explains.

I can feel my hackles rise, and I don't realize I'm making a face until Darren leans down to give me a kiss. "Don't be jealous," he says.

"I'm not jealous," I retort quickly and noticing Darren's wolfish grin, I scowl even more.

"I'll be home later, and we can have dinner," he offers, heading towards the door. "Lottie will be happy to see you."

Lottie is at the lake house? I'm excited but also a little nervous because I don't know how she feels about me leaving, especially since I didn't say goodbye.

I sit up in bed, smashing down the comforter with my arms as Darren exits the room. "I am not jealous!" I call after him.

Maybe just a little.

Now I can't go back to sleep, so I throw the blankets off and look for my luggage. I didn't have time to unpack anything, so I pull out a change of clothes and walk out into the living room.

I don't see Lottie in the kitchen, but there's a plate of scones on the island and a discarded cup of coffee that must have been Darren's. I shake my head and dump it in the sink. The pot is still warm, so I help myself to a cup and walk over to the patio to peer out at the meadow. It's full of wildflowers and looks so different without snow. The trees are lush and green, and the small fishing boat sits in the water, no longer covered for winter.

I notice some of the family pictures have been removed from above the fireplace and the artwork along the hall is missing, too. It seems Darren has been making changes while I was gone.

I hear noises coming from the library and make my way further down the hall, where Lottie and a young boy are packing up some books.

"Evangeline!" Lottie claps her hands together as soon as she notices me. "Come here, come here! It's so good to see you." She rubs my arm.

I tilt my head in the direction of the young boy who's diligently tapping a box closed.

"This is Noah, my grandson," she introduces us.

"Noah, this is Mrs. Walker."

For once, I don't flinch at the use of the surname. Although I can't help but run my thumb over my empty finger.

"Nana said if I helped with the boxes, she'd let me go swimming in the lake." Noah looks to be around eight years old and has the same brown eyes and wide toothy smile as Lottie. I knew she had sons, but she never talked about her grandchildren.

"Is that safe?" I ask skeptically.

"Darren used to jump off the pier at the same age as Noah, but I make him wear a life jacket."

"What's all this?" I point to some of the empty bookshelves and boxes that litter the library.

She turns her attention to Noah. "There are a couple boxes over there that need to be taped closed. Remember to use double. We don't want the box to fall open." She hands Noah the tape before she straightens up. "Darren thought it was time to make some changes around here."

"I see that." It should be a good thing, but it's oddly disorienting. The last time I was in here, Darren was studying for the Bar exam. His papers and books had been strewn all over the desk. I remember the room looking dark and masculine, but with the bookshelves starting to empty and the paintings removed, it brightens up the space.

"Where would you like to start?" Lottie asks, looking at me skeptically.

"Excuse me?" I ask.

"Darren said you would be taking over the redecorating." Lottie must see the confusion on my face. "Oh, I see he didn't get around to telling you, then."

I laugh. "No. I barely had a chance to talk to him before he left this morning. I don't really know much about decorating." I look around the room. "What does Darren want?" I ask.

"Darren will like whatever you pick out. This is your home, too. It's about time you made it your own."

It's my home, too, but it doesn't feel that way.

"Has Darren been staying here the whole time I've been back in Arizona?" I wonder.

"He travels back and forth between here and Georgetown," she offers, and I help her fit a few more books into one of the boxes.

I look over at Noah, who has managed to make a fort with the boxes and a throw blanket from the nearby couch.

"Noah James!" Lottie pulls out the middle name card and Noah peeks his head out from the blankets.

"That is not your blanket," she scolds, and Noah's face falls. He seemed pretty proud of his architecture skills.

"It's alright, Lottie. He can use the blanket," I offer softly.

Lottie nods with a smile. "You're putting it back where you found it." She points a stern finger at him, and he gives her a devilish smile before dipping back into the fort.

Now that we are semi-alone, I look at Lottie thoughtfully. "I missed you," I admit.

"I knew you wouldn't stay away for long."

Noah pokes his head out of the fort. "You said you would take me swimming."

"Go put your suit on."

Noah rushes out of the room, and I hear him stomping on the stairs to the second floor.

"I've never seen a kid run so fast," I laugh, pulling the blanket from the fort and folding it back onto the sofa.

"When you ask him to do chores, he's a sloth," Lottie jokes and we leave the office together laughing.

"Would you like to go down to the lake with us?" she offers. "It's a beautiful day."

It's tempting, because the lake looks so inviting with the sun reflecting off it, but I'm sure it's only warm enough for a kid not to complain.

"I need to go into town and get some things. Do you know if Darren left the car?"

"You can take mine. I don't need to go anywhere," she offers while shuffling through her purse on the counter until she produces a set of keys.

"You sure you don't mind?" I take the keys from her.

"I've got my hands full," she motions to the steps as Noah bounds down them wearing swimming trunks with sharks on them. "But if you want to pick up something for dessert tonight, that would be great."

"Oh, sure."

I watch as Lottie takes Noah out to the lake. He grabs her hand while they walk through the meadow to the dock and it pulls on my heartstrings a bit. It make's me miss my grand-mother as I watch Lottie pull a life jacket from the boat. Noah's practically bouncing on the balls of his feet while she straps it on. I can tell the minute it clicks into place because he bolts down the pier like a racehorse being let out of the gate and then cannonballs right off the edge.

As soon as I get dressed and grab another of Lottie's scones, I set off into town.

It's a beautiful spring day and there's not a cloud in the sky as I walk down the block. Across the street is a bakery, and I take note to stop there on my way out.

I open the door to The Vintage Vault and a middle-aged woman with a kind smile greets me.

"Can I help you find something?" she asks.

The store looks packed, and nothing seems to be organized in any sort of order. "I'm looking for something I can wear to events," I try out.

The woman looks me over. "We don't have anything designer in here." She clasps her hands together. "I like to describe our clothes as casual chic," she explains.

"That's perfect," I exclaim, and her mouth turns up into a huge smile.

"Ok, well, let me pull a few items for you." She sets to rummaging through the racks excitedly while I start flicking through some of the dresses up front.

A few of the shirts she pulls aren't really my style, but she shows me a floral dress that buttons on the top with a belt at the waist. I hold it up to myself in the mirror and fall in love with it.

"That'll look pretty on you," she says, and then stares at me a little longer in the mirror.

"Do you have a dressing room?" I ask, and she points me towards the back.

As soon as I have it on, I exit the dressing room so I can use the full-length mirror. It fits perfectly, and I adjust the belt so it's facing the right way. In the mirror, I catch the woman staring at me again with a curious expression.

I've been here almost an hour, and I'm still the only one in here.

"I put some more items on the back of the door for you," she calls to me.

I finish trying on a few more things and take them up to the register.

She looks like she wants to say something but stops herself. I look down to make sure I've buttoned my blouse and zipped my jeans, but all is well.

She rings up my items and before handing me the bag, she finally says, "Aren't you Darren Walker's wife? The one who's running for Congress?"

I wasn't expecting anyone to recognize me. "Yes, Evangeline."

"It's so nice of you shop in here," she continues, and I chew on my lip. I don't understand why anyone would care if I shopped in their store.

I hand her a few bills. "It's a great shop, and thank you for helping me find some things," I beam.

She stops me before I get to the door.

"I just meant that you could have shopped anywhere," she laughs nervously and then smiles at me. "People can say they care about the community all they want, but actually being part of it is something very different, ya know?"

I exit the store and almost run right into another lady about to enter. I'm about to apologize when she snaps a picture of me.

"Excuse me?" I shield my eyes from the flash.

"Barb Henderson from the Clarksville Caterwaul," she introduces herself, sticking out her hand which I reluctantly take, and she shakes it vigorously.

She must see the confusion on my face because she points to the woman inside the shop.

"Kathy Bennett, she owns The Vintage Vault." She leans in conspiratorially. "She's also my cousin, but I assure you there's no conflict of interest."

"I'm sorry, but what is all this?" I point to her camera.

"She called me and said Darren Walker's wife was in her thrift shop buying clothes."

"And this is news because?" I tilt my head, urging her further.

"Well, truth be told, we don't get a lot of news around here," she says as if that's a shocker. "But it's not every day that a billionaire shops at a thrift store."

I'm not a billionaire. It's Darren's family's money.

I must be staring too long because she goes on, "Maybe if people see you shopping here, they'll shop too." She shrugs.

It's then that I notice how empty the street is and how easily I found a parking spot. Next to The Vintage Vault is a vacant space that I hadn't noticed earlier.

"I like thrift shops," I compliment. "There are lots of treasures that you can't find at a regular department store."

"Can I quote you on that?" Barb calls after me as I cross the street to the bakery.

12

Participation Award

Darren

"Lottie's not having breakfast with us?" Evangeline asks, taking a seat on the deck and admiring the bowl full of fruit and assorted pastries she left for us.

"Noah's up at the crack of dawn, so they ate earlier," I explain.

"You should have woken me," she sounds offended.

I laugh. "I didn't want to get my head cut off."

She rolls her eyes. "I'm not that bad, am I?"

"I think it's absolutely adorable that you're not a morning person."

She brings the cup to her lips, peering over it with a smile.

"I hope you don't mind that Noah's here. Lottie's been bringing him for a couple weeks in the summer ever since he was little," I explain.

"Of course not. He's sweet, and it's been nice to have the company," she implies, scooping fruit onto her plate.

"I know I've been busy, but it won't always be like this," I offer.

"Yes, it will. Especially if you win."

"We'll figure it out." I offer a small smile while pouring cream into my coffee.

"Did you find an interior designer?" I change the subject.

"Rustic Charm Designs," she answers. "They're coming by today."

I lift an eyebrow and laugh. "That sounds interesting."

"They're local. I thought it would be nice."

"Whatever you want," I say, flipping through *The Post*.

"It's not what I want, Darren. This is," she pauses. "I don't know why you want to change everything."

"I want this to be *our* home. If I win, we'll be staying here a lot and—" I sigh, wanting to find the right words but failing. "I just want it to be ours."

She opens her mouth to counter, but the patio door slides open.

"Explain to me why your wife is shopping at a thrift store?" Rausch asks, tossing down a copy of a newspaper.

"Sitting right here." Evangeline raises a hand, but Rausch ignores her.

"I'm trying to have breakfast with my wife," I protest.

"This isn't a nine-to-five job. Not that you know what that is, either," Rausch gripes.

Sighing, I pick up the paper. "I think the better question is why you're reading the Clarksville Caterwaul?" I toss it back down.

"And you gave them a quote?" Rausch turns his attention to her.

I raise an eyebrow and stifle a laugh.

"Do you think this is funny?"

"No, but come on." I pick up the paper again to skim the article and then look across the table in amusement. "Did you really say there are lots of treasures that you can't find at a department store?" I ask, trying and failing to hold in my amusement.

"You can't just go talking to the press," Rausch accuses. "Not before we've had time to prep you."

Evangeline throws her napkin onto the table. "Barb ambushed me. What was I going to do, be rude?"

"Barb?" Rausch throws up an eyebrow. "We're on a first name basis with the press?"

"She and Kathy are cousins," she says absently.

"Excuse me, but who is Kathy?" Rausch probes.

"She owns The Vintage Vault. I don't know how she knows who I am, but she's the one who called Barb," Evangeline says, looking contemplative.

"I know exactly how she knows who you are." Rausch picks a piece of fruit from the dish. "That little stunt the other day." He pulls out his phone from inside his suit jacket.

This time it's from a reputable paper, and on the screen is a picture of Evangeline and I kissing.

"Did I not tell you that this would happen?" Rausch finally takes a seat.

Noah comes running out onto the patio. "Uncle Darren, how does a yeti feel when he gets the flu?"

I place a finger to my lips, pretending to think hard. He bounces on his feet excitedly as if he can't wait to spill the answer.

"I don't know. How does he feel?" I ask.

Noah laughs. "Abominable."

"That was a good one."

"There you are. I hope he wasn't interrupting." Lottie steps onto the patio a bit breathless and gathers Noah into her arms while he struggles to get away.

"Not at all, in fact he was providing us with some entertainment."

"Was he now?" Lottie leans down and pinches his cheek.

"Uncle Darren, are you going to take me in the boat?"

"Not today." Noah's face falls, and Rausch looks annoyed.

"But this weekend, if Uncle Rausch lets me out of work early."

Rausch grumbles while adjusting his suit jacket.

"Yay!" Noah manages to move his hands out of Lottie's grasp.

"Okay, come on now, we still have some work to do," Lottie smiles and scoots Noah back into the house.

Rausch stands up. "Don't mislead the boy by having him think I'm his uncle," he grumbles.

I laugh. "It's a term of endearment."

"I don't want to be endearing," he gripes.

I look across the table at Evangeline. My wife. She's still in her pajamas. The collar of her white fluffy robe is pulled tight around her neck and the belt secured around her waist. If we didn't have a houseful, I would enjoy unraveling her and tasting more than the breakfast on the table between us.

I clear my throat. "This is more coverage than I've had in weeks." I set my coffee mug down triumphantly.

"The point is that we need to be a united front when dealing with the press because it can quickly get out of hand," Rausch continues.

"I don't disagree."

"From what I saw the other day the economy isn't doing these small towns any favors, and isn't that Darren's platform, revitalizing tourism amongst other things?"

Rausch turns his head. "Well, someone's been paying attention."

"I can do better things with my time than *redecorate*," she says pointedly.

"Well, that may be my cue to leave." Rausch stands and checks his watch. "I have a meeting with the director."

"Are you producing a movie I don't know about?"

"We spoke about this," he pronounces. "The TV ad."

I look at him blankly.

"Seriously, Darren, sometimes I wonder if you hear anything I say." Rausch gathers his things and adjusts his tie.

"I'll ride in with you, just give me a few minutes." I stand, finishing off my coffee.

He nods but before he shows himself out, Noah catches him by the front door. "Uncle Rausch, what is black and white and red all over?" he asks with a huge smile on his face.

Rausch gives him an indignant look. "That's easy, a newspaper."

Noah laughs. "No, it's a zebra with a sunburn."

Rausch is about to protest when Lottie catches up to him. "He got a joke book from the library for his summer reading," she explains.

"If I read five books this summer I get a coupon for a free ice cream cone at Sally's Sweets," Noah says proudly.

"And joke books count?" Rausch inquires.

Noah nods his head vigorously.

"I'll never understand this *participation award* generation."

Lottie hits the door shut with her hip after Rausch steps through it, and takes Noah upstairs.

"I thought I'd leave you the car so you can run errands," I offer to Evangeline and then lean over the table to grab the last strawberry. "You know you don't have to shop at thrift stores," I add with amusement.

"I didn't want to spend a lot of money."

"I doubt you could put a dent in the bank account, but you could certainly try," I smile ruefully.

"I'm not talking about *your* money; I'm talking about mine."

"You're my wife. What's mine is yours." I gather my empty dishes and head inside.

"You don't need to get a ride from Rausch," she says, following behind me with the rest of the plates.

"You need a car. Pick out whatever you want." I set my

dishes in the sink and Evangeline grabs them. She rinses each one before putting them in the dishwasher.

"Lottie has enough to do," she explains and then turns back around, leaning against the sink.

"Here's my credit card. Pick out a car," she mocks. "As if it's that easy."

I cage her against the sink. "It is that easy. I have money. Lots of it."

She looks up at me through her bangs.

"You have no idea how much I want to play hooky today," I tell her, and pull at the ties of her robe, letting it fall open to reveal her tank top and sleep shorts.

She wraps her arms around my shoulders as I lean down to kiss her, tasting coffee on her tongue, but she feels different, not committed, not as eager as she usually is.

"Surely two people kissing isn't too scandalous for Noah?" I suspect that's the reason for her hesitation.

She holds onto me, searching my eyes, and I feel a worrisome pull in my stomach.

"It's not that." She fidgets with the collar of my shirt and the sound of a loud, aggressive horn cuts through the air.

I groan and then jump again when the horn sounds a second time. I curse, letting her go.

"You better get going before he leaves without you," she smiles, patting my chest.

"Would that be a bad thing?" I tease, kissing her again, and this time she yields. I lean my forehead against hers as I hear Noah bounding down the stairs.

"Come pick me up later." I smile against her mouth.

"Ewwwwww," Noah exaggerates as he enters the kitchen and I laugh, looking over at him. "Just a couple years buddy, and you might feel different about kissing someone."

"I doubt that," he says, rolling his eyes.

I feel my phone vibrate and pull it out to see a text from Rausch to get my ass moving.

13

Dare for Change
Evangeline

On every street corner on the way to pick up Darren is a sign with his face on it.

Dare for change.

When I finally make it into Lynchburg, I turn down Main Street and look for an empty spot. I take my time walking down the block looking in shop windows for inspiration. When Ethan from Rustic Charm Designs came earlier, he asked what my vision was, and I didn't have one.

Darren wanted me to change it, to make it *our* home, but the problem was... I didn't know what that should look like, and no amount of paint colors or flooring options could answer that for me.

I didn't have an unrealistic expectation of what it would be like coming back. I didn't think that I would show up at his rally and everything would magically be okay. That's part of the reason it took me so long to come back in the first place.

I love Darren.

I love the person he's become.

But he feels out of reach, even though he's right in front of me. As I stand in front of the campaign headquarters looking through the window, I watch him with his staff, so easy with his smile, and casual with the way he sits on the edge of a desk talking passionately with his hands. Then I see the person he's with and the way she lays her hand on his arm and leans against him as she laughs at something he says.

Angie.

I open the door and walk through the maze of desks and veer out of the way as volunteers pass by. Stacks of signs lean against the wall and phones ring incessantly.

When Darren notices me, he smiles and then Angie follows his gaze, removing her hand from his arm.

"Evan, you remember Angie."

"Yes, nice to see you again." I tuck a piece of hair behind my ear and stand awkwardly between them.

"Are you ready to go?" I ask expectantly.

"Oh, you didn't have to come all this way, I could have given him a ride home." Angie smiles.

I lift my eyebrows. "I bet…"

"We were talking about the article in the Caterwaul," Darren explains.

"Oh, am I in trouble again for speaking out of turn?" I inquire in a not-so-teasing tone.

"No." She laughs. "Dare was just saying you should do more interviews. You were a hit. The community loves how down to earth you are."

"*Dare* said that?" I slide my eyes to him.

"And this must be the dress."

"Yes, it is." I straighten and look her in the eye.

I can't help but notice how at ease she is, and I feel a bit out of my element. No doubt she's smart and connected or Darren wouldn't have hired her.

"Are you going to be taking a more active role in the campaign now that you're back?"

"I'm sure you'll be seeing more of me around here."

"I have a few things to finish up," Darren announces, loosening his arm from around me. "If you want to wait in my office, I'll only be a few minutes."

My hand lingers on Darren's shoulder. Darren angles his head towards me as I move beside him.

"It was nice to see you again, Angie." I nod in her direction politely.

When I strut towards the office, I know his eyes are on me and *not* Angie.

Rausch stands in front of a map full of red and blue pins indicating which area is heavily leaning towards one party or the other. Right now, there are more red than blue.

"Darren's not doing well, is he?" I guess, and Rausch turns around.

"When voters don't know you, they don't trust you," he explains. "That's why we organized the rally in the park."

I lean against the desk and cross my arms over my chest.

"You look like you have something to say," Rausch runs a hand through his hair, smoothing down a few stray pieces.

"Darren's not used to losing."

"You came back for a reason. If you're not fully committed, then you need to make a decision, because Darren's heart needs to be in it to win," Rausch cajoles.

"I'll become a public figure if I commit fully, and that's a dangerous place for me to be," I admit.

"Do you doubt that when I said I would do everything in my power to protect you, that I could do it?"

"I don't want to be forever looking in the rearview mirror. If it isn't Langley, it'll be someone else."

"Just how many senators are there in your closet?" he asks with a cynical smile.

"Not as many as you'd think. Besides, Langley's different."

"How so?" He crosses his arms over his chest and settles in.

"He's much like Kerry in a way."

Rausch furrows his brow.

"He married into money and had to climb his way to where he is, but unlike Kerry, Langley climbed by stepping on those beneath him."

"And you think that's what set them apart?" he queries.

"Langley's insecure about whether he really belongs, and people who are scared do unpredictable things to protect themselves," I further explain.

"You think you know Kerry by just meeting him once?" Rausch challenges.

"You knew him best, didn't you?" I eye him, seeing the slight tic in his jaw.

He doesn't answer me, but he doesn't have to.

"Kerry didn't want people to know about where he came from, and he went to great lengths to hide that. So no, I don't doubt that you could protect my past from the press because you've already proven you *can* do that. The question is whether you *should*."

Rausch takes a seat, clasping his hands in his lap, and looks into the bullpen where Darren is still working with Angie.

"You remind me of Merrill," he observes, which gets my attention.

"You don't have to blow smoke up my ass, Rausch. It's not me you have to get over the fifty yard line, it's Darren."

"And you think you're nothing like Merrill," he chuckles.

"Don't tell me, she used the word ass while in conversation with you, but in a different context?" I grip the edge of the desk and cross my ankles.

"She didn't like me either at first."

"Shocker," I roll my eyes while drumming my fingers against my forearm, wondering what's taking Darren so long.

"I'm not the enemy, but neither is being the representative for the fifth district of Virginia," Rausch insists. "Do you think it was easy for Merrill to lose Kerry to The Hill?" he proposes.

"Is that the only thing she lost him to?"

He scowls. "She knew exactly what she was getting into when she married him."

"I did too, but then I fell in love with Darren, and I intend to keep him," I narrow my eyes. "Especially when he wins."

Rausch eyes me like he's performing a dissection.

"If you think I'm not in this to win, you're mistaken." I reassure him. "Just tell me what I need to do."

Darren enters the office and Rausch rubs his palms against his thighs before standing. He looks as though he can feel the tension between Rausch and me.

"Production starts Monday for the TV ads," Rausch announces, and Darren makes a face.

"We've talked about this." Rausch gets his attention as he finishes shoving papers into his bag.

He turns from the desk and leans against it. "I don't like mudslinging."

"Jordie Calhoun won't have a problem pointing out your weaknesses," Rausch counters.

He nods, but still hands him the notes. "Take out anything personal."

Rausch takes the paper reluctantly. "You know he won't be as gracious."

"What's he going to run?" I question, feeling uneasy.

"Nothing about you," Darren answers, giving me a reassuring smile.

"He likes to point out my lack of experience in his campaign ads, and"—he lifts an eyebrow—"my privilege."

"He means to say that Jordie likes to play up his family values and that Darren was partying and getting arrested for public indecency," Rausch answers for him.

Darren rubs the back of his neck with an embarrassed smile.

"Yes, we can all agree I'm the antichrist." Darren throws his hands up, half joking.

"Why can't we just come out and tell people who I am?" I blurt out.

"That you're my wife?" Darren counters, his eyes narrowed.

"You know what I mean. About my past."

Both Darren and Rausch's heads turn and it's comical as they mirror each other's expressions.

"You're joking," Rausch chides.

"No, I'm not," I offer. "It just makes sense."

"That's like cutting off the legs of a racehorse before the race even starts," Rausch argues, and judging by the expression on Darren's face, he might agree.

"While that's a particularly lovely metaphor," I say sarcastically, "if you rip the Band-Aid off now, you won't have to worry about it later."

"Who says the Band-Aid even needs to come off? I have it handled," Rausch quips.

I look to Darren for backup, but he stays silent.

"Let's put a pin it." Darren grabs his laptop bag, slinging it over his shoulder.

"I'll email you the talking points for the ad over the weekend," Rausch calls after him, and I follow him out of the office.

"Have a good night, Angie," he smiles as we pass by her desk, and she beams back.

"Goodnight. And it was nice to see you again, Evangeline!" she calls after me.

The walk to the car is quiet and I occupy my mind by window shopping.

"Did something happen with the decorators?" Darren asks, and his question rubs me the wrong way.

"No," I answer in a clipped tone, tossing him the keys.

He slides behind the driver's wheel but doesn't start the car.

He starts to say something, but I interrupt him.

"I'd like to start working back at the charity," I tell him. "I mean to take my place as chairwoman of the foundation."

"I thought you felt out of place on the board?" he asks.

"Let's put a pin in it," I say with sarcasm.

Darren hesitates for a moment but then he jams the car in gear, and we drive in silence the entire way back to the lake house. It's the longest twenty minutes of my life.

As soon as the car stops, I get out and slam the door behind me. Instead of going in the house, I walk along the path that goes through the side yard and out to the dock. I need some space, but Darren follows me. I can hear him breathing heavily the whole way.

"Are you embarrassed by me?" I whirl around as soon as we're out of earshot from the house.

"Of course not!"

I cross my arms over my chest and turn towards the lake. The breeze tosses my hair around my shoulders and causes ripples in the water.

I make a disbelieving noise.

He sighs heavily. "Telling people about your past comes at a cost," he contends.

"It'll cost you votes," I say for him.

"You should know by now I'm not worried about votes," he raises his voice. "You left because you didn't want your past to interfere and now you want to tell the world?"

"Because it's different now," I try to explain, looking at him. "I'm back. I'm your wife and I don't want to be hidden like some secret."

I brush my thumb over the empty place where my ring should be.

"You're not a secret that needs to be hidden." He reaches for me but I back away.

"Are you afraid to go against Rausch?" I challenge him.

"That's insulting." He rears back.

"Then what?" I make him look at me by standing in his line of sight.

"I'm not afraid of what it will cost *me*," he says, and then looks past me to the lake.

"I can handle Jordie pointing out all *my* flaws, *my* lack of experience, and *my* many indiscretions." He pauses and his gaze settles on me. "But I don't know how to handle criticism of *you*."

Suddenly, I'm at a loss for words.

"Anonymity is a gift, Evan. Don't take it for granted."

"I think it might be a little late for that, don't you think?"

"I don't have time for this." He lets out a frustrated breath. "If you haven't noticed, I'm not doing so well in the polls and the support I thought I would have from the rotary club doesn't seem to be panning out..." he leaves the sentence hanging.

"You're still angry with me."

"Yes, I'm angry!" he admits, raising his voice. "I don't want to be, but I am."

I wanted him to admit it but now that he has, his words sit on my chest like the weight of a piano.

"You broke my fucking heart!" He yells.

"I know," I admit, and we stand in silence staring at each other. I take a step forward. "I don't want to be a problem you have to solve."

He reaches for me. "You're not a problem. You're a solution. You've always been the solution."

I pull back and look up at him through my lashes. "Where's my ring, Darren?"

He gives me a devilishly handsome smile. "I'll get you a real ring, a proper ring."

"I want *my* ring," I demand, and risk sounding like a petulant child.

He digs into his pocket and pulls out his keys. He removes the cheap band from the keyring and places it on my finger.

"You had it in your pocket all this time?" I ask indignantly.

He shrugs, annoyingly flippant while I've been wondering this whole time when he was going to give it back to me.

"You're an asshole." I push hard on his chest. Before he realizes what's happening, he's falling backwards into the lake.

I place my hand over my mouth, but I can't muffle the laughter.

When he surfaces, he shakes the hair out of his face. He smiles, looking past me and I feel someone push hard, and I lose my balance.

"Noah!" I yell, just before I hit the water.

I surface, sputtering water from my mouth and trying to push my hair out of my face. "It's the middle of summer. Why is this water so cold?!" I fume, hitting the surface with my arms. "Are you laughing at me, Darren Walker?"

He pulls me to him.

"You look really good wet."

I feel my anger ebb away and brush my nose against his as I look at him through my wet lashes. He presses his lips to mine and I thread my fingers through his hair. Deepening the kiss, I forget that we have an audience until I hear Noah yell, "Ewwwww!"

14

Be A Good Wife
Evangeline

"I have to leave," I whisper and give Darren a peck on the lips.

"Baby, come on. I've already punished Noah for pushing you in," he says sleepily.

"You took him out for ice cream." I laugh, and he gives me a wolfish grin.

He opens his eyes and pulls me back into the bed. "Five more minutes," he insists, grabbing my ass and pulling me further into him, where I feel his hard cock press into me.

"There's a board meeting this morning," I tell him while trying to untangle myself from the sheets.

"Didn't I already prove I could make you come in less than five?" he raises a cocky eyebrow.

"You did, but why would you want to when you can have me for hours when you come back to Georgetown?"

"That is definitely something worth waiting for." He smiles against my lips and releases me. "But I've never been a patient man.

"Audrina will be happy to see you," he says.

I flop back onto the bed and close my eyes.

"Don't tell me you're scared of Audrina?" Darren teases, rolling over and propping himself up by his elbow.

"I'm not scared."

"Liar." He pokes me and I laugh.

"Mildly intimidated," I offer. "I don't know what to say to her," I admit.

"Tell her the truth."

Maybe I'm all talk about telling the world that I used to be an escort because the thought of facing Audrina and Bethany with the news makes me queasy.

"Tell her that your grandmother died, and you had to put your family affairs in order," he corrects and then shrugs. "What? It's truth adjacent."

"Truth adjacent," I grumble. "You really are a politician now."

He pulls me closer to him. "I'll go with you."

"You have an ad to film," I remind him. "I'd stick around just to see them put makeup on you, but I'd miss the meeting," I tease.

"Makeup? No one said anything about makeup."

"You can't be on camera with a shiny nose." I touch the tip of his nose.

He grimaces. "This makes filming an ad even less appealing."

"You'll do great, I'm sure, and just think of how many voters you'll reach."

"I don't want you to drive all that way by yourself."

"If you'd let me take the helicopter…"

He cuts me off with a look.

"The chances of the same thing happening to me that happened to your parents are very small," I try to reason.

"No. End of discussion," he declares, turning me over

onto my back, pressing the weight of his body over mine, and I concede.

The sound of his commanding voice vibrates through me and I wiggle under him as he draws my arms over my head.

I wrap my legs around his waist and feel his erection press into me. He kisses my temple and works his way down my jaw.

"You're going to make me late," I insist a bit noncommittally.

"Do I need to tie you to the bed?" he groans against my neck, and I swallow hard at the thought of it.

My lack of protest causes him to lift his eyes to mine. He sits back on his heels, my legs still wrapped around him, and he drags a palm between my breasts and down the silky nightgown until it reaches my belly, which quivers under his touch.

We stare at each other in the silence with the early morning light filtering in through the drawn curtains. It makes the room look hazy.

"Five minutes." He looks at the clock on the bedside table and then back at me. "I think I'll take my time."

He retrieves the discarded tie from the nightstand.

"Darren." I really do have to leave, but with that look in his eyes and the tie gripped in his hand, I can't seem to make myself move.

He takes my wrists, and I stretch my neck to watch as he wraps the tie around them, careful not to pull it too tight, as he restrains me to the headboard.

With his lips close to my ear he says, "Now, be a good wife and try stay quiet."

I writhe beneath him and close my eyes as he drags his hand from my arm down the side of my body, his thumb brushing over my already hardened nipple. The bed moves as he shifts his weight and grips my hips.

His eyes become a lusty green as he takes me in and I wiggle beneath him. "Jesus, you look so fucking beautiful tied up like a present just for me," he breathes, and heat blooms in my stomach.

Slowly, he lifts the nightgown as if he's unwrapping me, pressing kisses to my belly and up my ribcage, leaving goose-bumps in his wake. He stops just below my breast and wraps his mouth around the tight bud of my nipple over the silk material. I lift my head to watch as his tongue darts out, wetting the fabric, pulling and sucking until my body is shaking and I'm begging him to relieve the ache that's formed between my legs.

How can such a simple thing cause my body to feel as if it's on fire? I've missed him so much.

Without even realizing, I'm moving my hips to the cadence of his tongue as he licks and sucks. I'm seeking out the hardness of his cock, wishing he were inside me as he worships each breast. As much as I wanted him to restrain me, I want to touch him, to run my fingers over his shoulder blades and down the hard ridges of his stomach until I hold his cock in my hand.

If I wanted to, I could slip my wrists through the loosely tied material, but when I pull, Darren lifts his eyes to meet mine and shakes his head.

"Do you want me to stop what I'm doing to you?" he asks in a low, rough voice that sends tingles down my spine.

I shake my head.

He leaves my nightgown bunched above my breasts and then works his way down my body. My chest rises and falls with each shuddering breath as he runs his tongue over my slit. Even through my panties it sets me on fire.

"You're wet for me," he says in a pleased tone.

I dig my foot into the mattress, trying to stay still. "Yes."

He rewards me by pulling my panties down enough that

he can kiss the sensitive skin just above my clit, and I love the tease just as much as I hate it. I lift my hips, urging him to pull them all the way off, and he nips at me.

Closing my eyes, I tip my head back into the pillow, my mouth dropping open as he obliges me by pulling my panties all the way off. I can feel his breath against me, and I shiver, suppressing another moan. I tilt my head so I can watch as he gazes down at me and all I can see are thick black lashes. His tongue darts out to wet his lips as if I'm a meal he's about to savor.

It's slow and wicked the way he laps at me, his tongue swiping at my clit with a torturous flick that only allows a jolt of pleasure to rip through me before it dissipates.

"Oh, God," I squeak out, my moans getting louder until he stops.

"I know it feels good, baby, but you have to stay quiet," he urges me.

I bite my lip when he sits back and slips his boxers down to reveal his hardened length dripping with precum. It pulses in his hand as he slides the wetness down his shaft. When he leans over me to press a kiss to my lips, he knows exactly what he's doing as his cock glides through my opening and I moan into his mouth.

"Darren, please," I beg.

All I want to do is wrap my arms around his neck and pull him to me but I can't and it's torturous. It's all too much. I fight to stay quiet while he runs his length back and forth, skimming over my clit, causing me to jump in response. I'm on the edge and I feel as if I'm teetering—fighting to stay in that sweet spot before I fall. I push my hips up to meet each stroke.

Just a little bit faster or a little more pressure and I'm there. I don't care if I look desperate or needy, I'm to the point where all modesty is buried.

I want my husband.

I want him badly.

He leans over me, his body weight grounding me as he pushes in. I let out a gasp, but I can't hold in my cries any longer. "Darren," I say, before his palm closes over my mouth and I scream into it.

15

Chairwoman
Evangeline

"*Y*ou must be excited to hear from me. You never answer on the first ring," Cleo exclaims.

"I've been busy lately, but today you happen to have good timing." I cradle the phone while juggling my coffee as I push through the glass doors of the office building.

"So does that mean you're not excited to hear from me?" she teases.

"I am glad you called because I'm about to do something really stupid or really brave," I tell her.

"This sounds like I might need to make some margaritas," Cleo declares, and I can hear the cabinets opening in the background.

"It's ten in the morning," I exclaim.

"Don't forget about the time difference. It's seven here," she laughs, and I can hear one of the cabinet doors slam.

"That's even worse!" I maintain indignantly.

"Relax, I'm just joking," she reassures. "Seriously though, what's got you in a twist?"

"Audrina Ellwood, among others," I explain, taking a sip of my coffee while I stop in front of the elevators.

"I thought the two of you were friends?" Cleo questions. "I mean, not friends like we are..."

"Of course not," I offer. "We're friendly. You know how it is with these ladies."

"No, actually I don't."

"You know what I meant," I sigh. "This whole thing is hard. I'm trying to figure out where I fit in here."

"You belong there just as much as anyone, Evan," she insists, giving me a little boost of confidence. "What's your plan?"

"I'm going to ask to take over the board," I state resolutely.

"Now that's what I'm talking about!"

"You don't think I'm getting ahead of myself?" I ask.

"Sounds like maybe *you* think that," she challenges.

"It's complicated." I bite my lip. "Rebecca Langley is on the board."

"Jonathan Langley's wife?" she questions. "Does she know about you?"

"No!" Jonathan most certainly would not have told her about me, but that doesn't mean she hadn't found out on her own.

I shake the thought from my mind and look up at the clock. "I have to go. I'll call you later." I shove my phone inside my purse and grab the next open elevator.

I race into the conference room to see Bethany placing a packet at each seat. There's no one else in the room, so I have a few moments to speak with her before the rest of the members arrive. I would have been here earlier if Darren hadn't distracted me. As soon as she sees me standing in the doorway, she sets the pile of reports down.

I wasn't sure how I would be received after leaving without a word, but the smile on her face is comforting.

"Evangeline," she exclaims, approaching me. She holds onto my arms as if inspecting me for damage. "It's so good to see you."

Instead of shying away from a hug, I hold onto her, thankful that she's not angry with me. Being in Darren's world is daunting enough but doing it without allies would be impossible.

"I'm sorry I left without letting you know," I apologize.

"Darren said your grandmother passed. I'm so sorry."

"Yes, thank you. I don't want you to think I don't finish what I start," I say.

"No one thinks that," she reassures me. "You should see Compton House," she exclaims. "Someone donated five million dollars. We've been able to pay off the mortgage, and we're making expansions. I can't wait for you to see it." She leads me over to the chairs.

"I would love to see it." I knew Bethany would see to it the money went to good use. I set my purse purposefully on the seat at the front of the table. "I was hoping that seat on the board was still available."

After all my trepidation, she gives me a wide smile, making me feel at ease. I know I don't have to ask for that seat because it's rightfully mine, being married to Darren, but I owe Bethany the courtesy. "There's always a seat on the board for a Walker," she says.

"Not just any seat." I take a deep breath. "I want Merrill's seat."

Bethany straightens. "Oh, I see."

"I want to talk to Audrina about it," I continue. "But…"

"You wanted to run it by me first," she finishes for me.

I smile because she understands. "I don't want to step on any toes."

"I can't speak for Audrina. She stepped in when Merrill passed," Bethany explains. "This was her way of honoring what Merrill built."

"The two of you were her oldest friends," I observe. "I want to be respectful because I understand what it means to both of you."

"I think Audrina will appreciate that." She slaps the last report down on the conference table just as Audrina and a few of the other board members enter the room.

"Evangeline!" Audrina gives me a hug. "It's so good to see you. I was sorry to hear about your grandmother. I hope everything is settled?"

"Yes, thank you. There's something I wanted to talk to you about." Bethany gives me an encouraging smile. "I know that you took over the charity for Merrill and you've done such a wonderful job, but I'd like the chance to take on that responsibility."

"I see," Audrina blinks. She sets her purse down on the conference table and smiles at a few more members who take their seats at the table.

Rebecca Langley enters the room. "Evangeline," she kisses my cheek. "I was so sorry to hear about your grandmother," she apologizes.

"I appreciate that." I respond by politely giving her hand a squeeze.

"Does this mean you're back?" She looks between Audrina and me.

I look to Audrina before responding. "Yes, if you'll have me."

"Oh, don't be silly. You've been missed, and you should see Compton House," Rebecca says excitedly.

"I've heard."

"We should go there today. After the meeting," Rebecca offers. "If you have time, of course. I was inspired by you." She goes on, to my surprise. "I've been helping out, finishing what you started with the clothing drive. We even started a mock interviews program. We've gotten volunteers from some local businesses."

I had no idea Rebecca was so interested in Compton House. "Of course," I relent. "I'm happy to hear that what I started was not only carried forward but expanded on."

Audrina interrupts by standing at the head of the table and calling the meeting to order. She stands at the front of the room, her silver hair perfectly pulled back into a low bun and wearing a designer dress. She certainly looks the part.

"We have a change of agenda," she announces, and I look across the table to Bethany. "Normally, we don't vote on committee members until next quarter, but this is a special election." She glances over at me. "Evangeline Walker would like to take over as chairwoman for the foundation." All eyes are on me.

A new chairwoman isn't something that Audrina can appoint, rather, it needs to be put to a vote. A vote from a board who barely know me.

"If you have something you'd like to say to the board before the vote, you may do so now," Audrina addresses me, and I feel grossly unprepared, but I stand anyway.

"Thank you," I say to Audrina, who steps aside while I take her place. "This foundation has come to be an unex-pected gift." I smile. "It gave me purpose when I needed it the most. I'm so glad to have been able to help so many women in need and I'd like the chance to do more and expand on the wonderful job that Audrina Ellwood has done." I pause, looking over at Bethany and Audrina. "I would like to think that Merrill would approve."

Audrina stands up and I move so she can take my place in front of the board. It's hard to tell what she's thinking.

"Let's take a vote. All in favor of Evangeline taking over the foundation, raise your hand."

Bethany raises her hand right away and I smile at her, thankful that I have at least one person on my side. I look around the table and to my surprise, Rebecca Langley raises her hand. A couple of the other board members start to raise their hands, and the few that don't cause a tie in the vote.

I look to Audrina for what to do in this situation, but then I realize she has a vote too. Her mouth tilts into a smile as she raises her hand.

"Add it into the record that Evangeline Walker has been voted in as chairwoman for the Abigail Pershing Foundation," Audrina declares.

"It's time to call this meeting to order," she announces.

I mouth the words *thank you*. She nods and then steps aside, motioning for me to take her place, which I do.

"Okay," I take a breath to get my bearings. "What's first on the agenda?"

"We have a few bids for the contractor work that's left so we need an approval from the board," Bethany pipes up.

I pull the report over, and we start going through the bids. I'm thankful for Bethany's help as I get used to this new role, but it feels good.

When the meeting concludes, I pack up my things and notice Audrina heading out.

"Hey," I reach out to her, and she stops in the doorway. We step aside so that the others can leave. "I wanted to thank you."

"It was the right thing to do," she insists, and although the smile on her face is perfectly pleasant, I'm not sure she's okay.

"I didn't have time to reach out to you before the meeting. I'm sorry if it came as a surprise," I apologize.

"To be honest, yes," she admits, and I brace myself. "I know how much effort you put in at Compton House, but... I think you're right."

I shake my head. "Right about what?"

She steps forward and touches my arm. I can see a twinge of sadness in her eyes. "Merrill would have liked to have you take over the board."

"How do you know that?" I inquire.

"Because I knew Merrill," she insists. "It was an honor to take over the board for her but it's time to hand that over to you."

Never did I think Audrina would make me cry.

"Sorry to interrupt," Rebecca interjects. "I wanted to know if you'd like to go to Compton House with me? I can show you all the wonderful changes."

"Oh, yeah. I'd love to," I confirm.

"I was also hoping you'd be able to go to lunch with me afterwards?" she asks.

How will I be able to look her in the eye, knowing that her husband hired me to sleep with him but was denied the pleasure, and hasn't forgotten about what he's owed?

16

Chickens Need Love Too

Darren

I toss the empty Styrofoam cup into the trash and run my hands through my hair.

"No, no, no, you're messing up your hair," Angie chastises.

I hold my hands up while she approaches me with a comb. "Geez, you make it sound like I've just been caught stealing condoms from the drugstore," I huff out.

"You didn't really do that did you?" she asks in a serious tone while trying to comb my hair back in place.

"My parents were Catholic."

"Well, let's hope the press doesn't get a hold of *that* story," she laughs, stuffing the comb back in her pocket as we walk back to the camera crew.

"Nope, but I saw this earlier," I huff out and hand her my phone, which displays an article with a picture of me from college.

Angie takes my phone, and she tilts her head as if trying to figure out what's going on. "Did you steal a dog?" She puts her hand over her mouth as if she's scandalized.

"That's Jack the bulldog, our school mascot, and it's a stat-ue." I snatch the phone back from her. "I'm not depraved."

"What were you doing with it?" she questions.

"It was a fraternity thing," I try to explain. "Never mind."

"Rausch is going to blow a gasket," she says.

"Speaking of Rausch, where is he?" I check my watch for the fifteenth time.

"He didn't tell you?" Angie inquires. "He had to drive back to Georgetown. He said he had some important business to take care of."

"More important than filming this tv spot that he insisted I do because he said I needed to reach a broader demograph-ic?" I challenge, hoping that my words travel all the way to Georgetown and hit Rausch over the head.

Angie shrugs and I let out a frustrated breath. I pull the notecards out of my pocket and go over the lines again.

"Let me write something up to counter the bad press. I'll run it by Rausch but maybe we can set something up with the dean, spin it like a fun prank, maybe get some good press for the non-profit law clinic?" she offers.

I can feel my anger start to ebb away. "That's a good idea, thanks," I tell her. When the director motions for me to start again, I face the camera and walk down the street.

"I'm Darren Walker, and I'm running for the House of Representatives for District five..."

"Why are you walking like you have a stick up your ass?" Alistair interrupts as he crosses the street, and the director throws his hands up.

"Cut!" he shouts.

"I do *not* walk like I have a..." I stop as I pass the screen where one of the assistants is replaying what we just filmed.

Shit. I am walking like I have a stick up my ass.

"Maybe if you imagine everyone naked it'll relax you a bit," Alistair offers, and for a second, only because I'm desperate, I think about trying that until I see one of the boom mic operators is about as old as Jesus, and I shake my head.

Fucking Alistair.

"That's for speeches, not filming a campaign advertisement." I check to make sure my tie is still straight. "What are you doing here anyway? Don't you have a job?" I question with a frustrated tone.

"I'm on business, if you must know."

"In Clarksville?" I laugh out the question.

"I was passing through on my way to Bullock. I didn't know I was going to be an extra in a film," he teases.

"What's in Bullock?" I inquire, grabbing a bottle of water.

"You don't want to know."

I raise my eyebrows.

"A chicken farm," Alistair concedes.

"You're right, I don't want to know." I down the water and throw it into the bin.

"We're losing light," the director barks. I'm sure he's frustrated with me, but that's too bad because I'm the one paying for this fiasco.

"You don't have to stick around," I tell Alistair.

"Oh no, I'm not missing this for the world," he laughs.

I get into position. "By the way, I don't think you'd last long even in a white-collar prison."

"What's that supposed to mean?"

"I know you're an animal lover, but I know you're not going to a chicken farm to liberate them."

"Chickens deserve love too," Alistair barks.

"Insider trading is serious," I warn him. "And I'm not representing you if you get busted."

"Hey," he says while backing away. "I'm just going there to make sure our investment is safe."

"Stay out of trouble. I have enough of my own," I wave him off.

"Oh, I've seen." Alistair pulls out his phone and attempts to show me something.

"If this is about Jack, I've already seen it. By the way, let's not forget who actually broke in and stole the statue."

"True, but I wasn't the one they took a picture of while trying to mount it," Alistair contends through fits of laughter.

"I was not mounting it. He was heavy and I was trying to scoot him—look it doesn't matter. That was,"—I do the math in my head and realize it wasn't really that long ago—"almost a decade ago," I say because it sounds better.

"That's not entirely accurate. Anyway, that's not what I was referring to."

He hands me the phone, and there's an article about my father speaking at the University of Arizona four years ago.

17

Would You Like A Cookie?

Evangeline

*R*ebecca Langley sits opposite me, a glass of wine in front of her and a beautiful salad that she's barely touched. Her dark hair is pinned in an elegant bun and she's wearing a flattering wrap dress that complements her light skin tone. She touches the white linen napkin to her lips, leaving a bit of red lipstick behind as she places it back on the table.

We've been talking so much about Compton House and plans for this year's charity gala that I've barely tasted my soup.

"This has really been nice," Rebecca exclaims. "You know, you should have dinner with Jonathan and I sometime." The mention of him causes the hair to rise on my arms. "I'm not much of a cook, and I usually meet him somewhere by the Capitol in between sessions."

I don't want to offend her but there's no way Darren could be in a room with Langley without losing his temper. "Darren's so busy we barely have time together. He won't be back in Georgetown until late tonight."

"How's the campaign going?" she asks.

"Well, I've never been at the center of one, so I don't know," I answer honestly.

Rebecca sits back in her chair, taking her glass of wine in hand. "I don't think I have to tell you about the intricacies of politics." She smiles and takes a sip.

I falter, trying not to assume her meaning.

"I mean, you strike me as someone who picks up on things quickly. Like you did with Compton House," she offers.

"Oh, yes." I take a sip of my water. "I guess I just threw myself into it because it was something I was passionate about."

"That's exactly what we need on the board. Audrina has done such a wonderful job taking over for Merrill but it's nice to have a new perspective."

"Did you know Merrill well?" I ask.

She looks taken aback.

"Of course," she says, and then her expression becomes contemplative. "There was a time when we were very close."

I would like to know more but I don't want to pry.

"Being a politician's wife isn't easy," she offers.

"I'm beginning to understand that." I scoff.

"Your life isn't private anymore," she explains. "The press doesn't care who they hurt." She sets her drink down and looks out the window.

"You sound like you have some experience with that," I persist, bringing her attention back.

"We all have. Darren grew up with it, being Kerry's son, but for us wives, it's different." She finishes her wine, and the waiter returns to refill it, but she places her hand over the top.

"That might be true, but he's not immune to the press running false stories or an opponent feeding information to the press about past transgressions," I imply, but her expression remains passive.

"If you ever need someone who understands, my door's always open."

I blow out a breath. "I might take you up on that."

The waiter drops off the check and Rebecca grabs it before I have the chance.

"You don't have to do that," I say.

"It's my pleasure. Besides, I'm the one who asked you to lunch," she smiles, placing her credit card in the billfold.

"Will you excuse me? I need to use the restroom." I head towards the back of the restaurant but before I get there I run into Rausch as he exits the gentlemen's cigar lounge. The annoyed look on his face suggests he wasn't in there for a relaxing afternoon cigar and malt liquor.

"I thought you were with Darren!" I say in surprise.

"I had unexpected business to take care of here," he explains, shoving his hands into the pockets of his dress slacks.

"What business is that?" I inquire, placing a hand on my hip.

"The kind that's none of yours," he says.

"Does Darren know you're here?"

"I don't have to run it by Darren wherever I go."

"That means he doesn't know then." I give him a satisfied smile.

He looks down at the expensive gold watch on his wrist. "I'm sure Angie's told him by now." His gaze travels over my shoulder. "Interesting choice for a lunch date." He raises an eyebrow.

"She's on the board for the foundation." I point out. "I was voted in today as chairwoman."

"Would you like a cookie?"

I give him a sour expression. "Usually, I can handle your lack of decorum, but you're especially ornery today. Is everything okay?"

He lets out a breath. "I apologize," he offers. "Congratulations, I know Darren will be happy about you taking over his mother's charity."

"You know, anything that concerns Darren or the campaign *is* my business."

"I've got it handled," he gripes.

I shake my head. "If you did you wouldn't look so worried. Is this about the article on Kerry's visit to Arizona?"

His expression darkens.

"I'm not the enemy," I say.

"Jonathan likes to play games."

"That's exactly why I think I should make a statement about my past," I explain.

"I'm good at my job because I handle the unpleasant things so that Darren can focus on winning," he explains.

"The focus should be on making a difference in the community," I insist.

Rausch moves a little closer to make room for a party to walk by. He lowers his voice. "And he cannot make a difference if he isn't elected. Which is what I'm trying to ensure."

"Ensure?" I question, my eyes wide.

"Do not insinuate that I'm doing anything underhanded."

I wave my hand to the lounge he just came from. "A dimly lit cigar lounge screams legitimate."

The creases on his forehead deepen.

"What aren't you telling me?"

"When Darren comes back to Georgetown, we should talk."

18

The Letter

Darren

I enter Johnny's Half Shell, an oyster bar near the Capitol Building. It's an industrial looking restaurant with an open ceiling and exposed ventilation. A long bench seat lines the wall, but I find my dinner date sitting at the bar. Rory Colton is a short man, with wide-set brown eyes, and a receding hairline. He doesn't look like the sort of man who could fill my father's shoes. I take the seat next to him and order a whiskey.

"I ordered a dozen oysters," he says by way of greeting. "I hope you're hungry."

"To say I was surprised that you called is an understatement." I take the glass in hand and twist it between my fingers before bringing it to my lips.

"I should have reached out a long time ago." He tucks a linen napkin into the collar of his shirt as soon as the waiter sets the oysters in front of him. They look plump and springy in their shells and when he offers me one, I decline.

He doesn't listen, placing one on my plate. "You should eat."

There's something about his tone that makes me pick up the shell and inspect it. I'm not opposed to oysters, but I close my eyes anyway while letting it slide down my throat, tasting the saltiness on my tongue.

I've been in the same room as Rory but never this close. I don't really know him, only *of* him.

"How are you liking my father's seat?" I inquire with a prickly tone while I use the napkin to pat my mouth.

Rory laughs, taking a drink of his gin. "I can understand your resentment. I imagine this isn't easy for you."

"You're part of the reason I'm running," I explain.

"Oh?" he questions, turning to look at me.

"I'm not going to fuck seniors out of their homes in order to build McMansions," I explain.

He reaches for the hot sauce unfazed and raises an eyebrow as if he's not sure what I'm talking about.

"The bill you voted against to freeze senior property taxes," I remind him. "One of those seniors is a volunteer on my campaign."

"Sometimes you have to sacrifice one thing in order to gain another. Your father understood that," he explains. "And perhaps you will too."

"Well, I'm not willing to sacrifice a bunch of seniors."

"I didn't invite you to dinner to squabble about things that can't be changed."

"Then let's get to the point, because my wife is waiting for me at home."

"Ok," he says with a bit of trepidation, and then leans in as not to allow anyone else to hear. "Am I correct to assume that you know about your wife's previous profession?"

"You'd better watch yourself, Rory," I warn.

We move away from each other as the waiter takes the billfold.

"I will assume that means you know."

"What do you want?" I fume.

"This is a professional courtesy, Darren, because despite how you feel about me, I admired your father," he insists.

I make a disbelieving noise.

"I've come to learn that the Post knows about your wife as well, and they're planning to run a story."

"Rausch would know if that were the case," I comment, more to myself than to Rory, because Rausch hasn't said anything to me about this. It dawns on me that he missed the taping of the ad for unexpected business in Georgetown. I wonder if that business was trying to suppress the article. Either way, he kept it from me and he didn't exactly accomplish anything.

"I don't doubt that, but there are some things out of even his control and the press can't turn a blind eye to this." He shakes his head.

"That's not something the press would stumble upon," I scoff.

"You'd be right about that," Rory confirms with a nod.

I don't need him to tell me who leaked it to the press because I already know.

The waiter approaches. "I hope you enjoyed everything," he smiles broadly.

Rory takes the billfold from the waiter with a smile and then scribbles his name on the receipt, slapping it closed.

My phone vibrates in my pocket, and I pull it out to make sure I don't miss a message from Evangeline, but it's from an unknown number.

Darren, it's your grandfather. Hoping we can talk.

I shove the phone back in my pocket. Jesus, what else can happen today?

"Always wonderful," Rory beams at the waiter as if he hadn't just dropped a bomb on my plate.

He slides off his chair and grips my shoulder. "If I were you kid, I'd get ahead of this."

I follow Rory onto the street. "That's what I have Rausch for."

Rory shakes his head. "Every strategist will tell you to deny until you can't deny anymore."

Which is exactly what Rausch has been doing.

"There's no proof," I tell him.

"We're not talking about a tabloid here. If the Post runs a story, it's because they have something solid," Rory confirms.

I pinch my forehead. Of course, I knew this was a possibility and we tried to be prepared as much as we could. "I'm not about to let them ruin my wife's reputation."

Rory looks at me with admiration. "You're a lot like your father. He was less worried about what they thought of him politically and more about who he was as a man." He offers me a small smile. "It's something lacking in Washington."

He didn't have to invite me to dinner, and he didn't have to warn me. Maybe I was too quick to judge him, and my dislike was more about my father's seat being empty in the first place, not who was taking it. If it wasn't Rory, it would have been someone else, and they still wouldn't have been deserving in my eyes.

I shake hands with Rory, and as we part ways I notice Langley crossing the street with his wife, Rebecca.

"Darren," Rebecca says excitedly. "Is Evangeline with you? I was just telling her earlier that we should have dinner sometime."

"Unfortunately, no." I try to sound polite but it's difficult when in the presence of the very man that threatens my wife's reputation. As Rory has said, I'm a lot like my father.

"I didn't know you were such good friends with Darren's wife." Jonathan looks a bit shaken, but he's hiding it well.

"Oh yes, we're on the planning committee together," she explains. "She's really taken on the role quite nicely and this year's gala will be quite something."

"When my wife puts her mind to something, there's no stopping her." I smile at Jonathan.

"Will you get us a table before the dinner rush?" Jonathan says to her.

She pats his arm. "If you wanted to be alone, all you have to do is ask," she laughs.

"Please tell Evangeline I missed her, and hopefully we can get together soon—the four of us. Wouldn't that be fun, Jonathan?" she smiles up at him and he pulls at his collar.

"Yes, of course."

Rebecca enters the, leaving Jonathan and myself in front of the restaurant. A cool evening breeze runs down the street.

"What kind of game do you think you're playing?" Jonathan accuses.

I laugh. "That's funny coming from you—planting stories about me and my wife!"

"Your platform is integrity and social justice, is it not?"

"The campaign is about me, not my wife," I remind him. "And if you think you're going to ruin my chances for election by exposing her past, which I might remind you involves you, then think again."

"Is that why your so-called wife is latching onto Rebecca?" he speculates. "She thinks I won't ruin you both just because they're friends?"

"Unlike you, my wife doesn't have any ulterior motives other than doing what's good for the foundation."

I push past him and walk down the street because if I had to look at him for even one more second, I might not have been able to control myself.

When I get home, Evangeline is in the office. Her hair is up in a messy bun, tendrils framing her face. She's in sweatpants and a tank top, bent over organizing one of the boxes of my father's law books. When she hears me enter the room she looks up and blows a piece of hair from her face.

Her expression is grave and for a moment I think she already knows what I'm going to say.

"You asked me to take over for Lottie," she says nervously, and motions to the boxes of law books I wanted to donate to the free clinic. "I was reorganizing the shelves, and the letter fell out of this book." She points to a book in front of her, *The Collected Works of Ralph Waldo Emerson*.

It's the first time I notice something in her hand.

"I think it's something you need to read," she explains, handing the handwritten note to me.

While spending time apart I've been able to put our marriage into perspective.

I think back to my ten-year-old self and try to remember if there was ever a time when my parents were separated, but I have only a vague recollection of the summer I spent with my mother at her family's estate in New Hampshire. I hadn't thought of that in such a long time, the memory hardly seems real.

I've come to terms with the fact that we are not the only two people in this marriage. If I'm being honest, I've known this for a while.

"My father was having an affair?" I don't realize I've said it out loud until Evangeline reaches over the boxes and touches my arm. She looks at me as if I'm someone to be handled carefully. Maybe I am.

Maybe I'm writing this letter so you can't talk me out of it but I've made a decision. I don't want a divorce. I believed in you the day I met you, and I knew you were going to do great things, just like I know it now.

It won't be a marriage in name only because we're partners in this. The three of us.

The most important thing is to protect our family.

Protect our family from what?

I set the letter on the desk.

"Evan," I must say her name in a way that causes her expression to turn into a different kind of worry. "I have something to tell you."

19

Political Wife

Evangeline

"*H*ave I ever told you how unbelievably sexy you look wearing my t-shirt?" Darren smirks, entering the kitchen where I have my laptop set up on the island and coffee brewing.

I smile and look down at Darren's Georgetown t-shirt hanging off one shoulder and sitting just at the tops of my thighs.

I kiss him. "Many times."

He looks at the screen. "Am I interrupting?"

"Just looking over the venues for the charity event we're planning."

"The annual event for the Foundation?"

"Yes, we're thinking of using the Smithsonian American Art Museum," I explain. "Their rooftop terrace looks beautiful. Rebecca and I are going to take a look at it today."

The mention of her name causes a slight tic in his jaw, but he shakes it off.

"I know it's awkward, but I enjoy her company, and she's helping to put together the gala."

"It's not an issue," he says, and I let it go.

"I quite liked the National Portrait Museum," he says coyly, not missing a beat.

"It's on the list," I smile.

"You know you can use the office if you want," he offers.

I look at him thoughtfully. "I know, it's just…" I pause. "It doesn't feel right."

Darren sighs, taking the seat next to me. "No matter what I change in this house it doesn't seem to extinguish them, does it?"

"Why would you want to?" I ask, closing my laptop. I'm not going to finish any work this morning.

"I was trying to make it my own, so it wasn't a constant reminder of what was lost, but rather what could be," he offers with a hopeful tone.

I swivel my chair towards him and place my hands on his thighs. His hair is still wet from the shower and his old t-shirt stretches across his shoulders. "You haven't said anything about the letter." I feel guilty that I'd even found it.

"I can't think about them, when all I can think about is you."

I lean against the sink and worry but I decide to let it go for now.

"You need to tell Rausch to set up a press conference."

He lets out a heavy sigh and joins me. "I'll have Angie set it up," he relents.

"Why Angie?" I question. "Rausch knows how to handle these things."

"Angie has a background in journalism. She may not be a tyrant like Rausch, but she knows what she's doing," he explains. "Rausch will just try and talk us out of it."

I nod reluctantly. "He won't be happy about it."

"He keeps things from me all the time. Besides, he works for me, Evan, not the other way around."

I nod.

"We can get ahead of this and I can finally put that *fuck* Langley in his place," he glowers.

"It needs to be me."

Darren's nostrils flare. "I'm not putting you through that."

"It's not your story, Darren. It's mine," I explain, and his eyes turn a golden color from the sun filtering through the kitchen window.

"Then you tell them *everything*."

I get his meaning, but I shake my head. "I won't give them a client list."

"Just Langley."

I slide past him and back to the island, placing my hands on the cool marble.

"Why wouldn't you want to expose him for the sleazebag he is?" Darren follows me.

"Rebecca."

His face falls.

"I can't do that to her," I explain.

Instead of being angry with me, he pulls me into a hug. His palms rub circles around my back in a soothing cadence.

He's silent for a few heartbeats before he nods.

"We'll do the press conference here and then drive straight to Clarksville for the lake house until things calm down," Darren explains. "I'll hire extra security so no one can access the property."

He grabs his phone and starts texting, his forehead creased with determination. I can't think of a person I trust more than Darren.

I place my hand over his phone and push it down.

"I don't want to be that kind of political wife. The kind that redecorates and plans parties without having something of my own," I explain. "Or one that hides out in a lake house."

"You don't know how bad it can get, and you have the charity."

I sigh and let go of the phone. I don't know if I can explain to him without sounding pathetic or jealous, but the mention of Angie having a journalism background was like an arrow hitting me in the most vulnerable part.

"I started something in school that I never got to finish," I explain. "And now that—well, now I have options that I didn't before."

I turn to face him, leaning against the sink.

"You were in school for journalism," he elaborates for me.

I nod. "I wanted to be an investigative journalist." I shrug, having felt that dream slip further away from me for years now.

"I thought journalism was my chance to do something good with my life." I sigh, knowing how naïve I sound.

"You *are* doing something good with your life," he insists.

"By being a Washington society wife?"

"You know you do more than that."

"It just feels very privileged to not have to worry about the things that the women at Compton House do." I press my lips together and look at him.

"You can do whatever you want. You can go back to school, get your journalism degree. There's nothing stopping you," he tells me, and I can see the conviction in his eyes.

"I'm not that same person anymore." I shake my head. "Journalism isn't what I thought it was," I say.

"I hate that being front and center for the ugliness of the press has ruined this dream you once had."

"It was ruined long before that," I say sadly.

He reaches for me, and I let him take me into his arms. "If you let me, I'll give you anything you want."

"I just want you."

I know he would support me with whatever I wanted. I'm just not sure I deserve it.

20

Press Conference
Evangeline

*N*erves hit as soon as I see how much press has showed up.

"We can turn around right now," he says, and I love him for it.

"Would you drive the getaway car?" I ask teasingly.

"Absolutely," he offers. "So long as you don't try to give me road head on an icy highway again."

I laugh. "Oh well, if that's how you feel about it then I won't ever do that again." I blink up at him.

"I didn't say *never*." He smiles right before kissing me.

"You're very good at distracting me," I grin against his lips.

"I'm glad it's working."

His arm snakes around my waist as we walk further into the room, just behind the line of sight of the press.

"You're still not going to tell me what this is about?" Angie asks Darren.

I step in. "No."

PAULA DOMBROWIAK

"But I don't understand. If it has something to do with the campaign…"

"We didn't want to risk having the subject leaked," I explain, and her eyes widen.

"I would never divulge campaign strategy," she insists.

"This isn't campaign strategy," I retort. "This is of a personal nature that you will never understand. That's a good thing," I reassure her, and Darren squeezes my hand.

"Understood," Angie concedes.

I peer into the room full of waiting press. "Is that all just press?" I ask.

"I called all the reporters on the list you gave me but word travels fast. There are a few more regional papers than I expected," she explains. "Is that a bad thing?" She looks between Darren and me.

"It's fine," Darren replies.

"Says you," I say nervously.

"The mic is live. All you have to do is flip the switch. I can moderate questions if you like?"

"No, it'll be fine," I tell her.

Before I take my place at the podium, Darren grabs my wrist, and I can feel my own rapid pulse. "Hey," he whispers, and I angle my head so I can look at him.

He doesn't say anything else, but he doesn't have to. There's a whole conversation in his eyes: I don't have to do this.

I might be nervous but I'm not backing out.

Darren lets go of my hand and I stride across the room to the podium. Angie brings the room to order, and I set the speech I wrote onto the raised surface below the mic. I brought it in case my nerves made me forget, but I don't need notes to tell my own story.

I clear my throat and the mic picks up the feedback. As I look out at the sea of reporters packed into the room, I catch a glimpse of dark hair and pale eyes.

Rebecca Langley.

What is she doing here?

I didn't think there would be anyone here I knew. Telling a room full of strangers is easier than telling the people you care about.

I suck in a breath and smile. "Thank you for coming." I grip the edges of the podium. "I'm sure you're wondering why we called you here today, so I'll get right to the point. My name is Evangeline Walker, but before I was married to Darren, I was Evangeline Bowen, and I worked for a high-end escort service."

21

Cats Out of the Bag

Darren

"*I* was handling it," Rausch says.

"Well, what a great job you did," I say.

"Darren," Evangeline warns, and my eyes snap to hers momentarily, but I'm too angry to listen.

"It's fine. Let him have his hissy fit," Rausch says.

"You think this is a hissy fit?" I ask indignantly. "I don't like secrets. I've had enough of them!"

"I've been forthcoming with you about everything that matters," he demands.

"Everything that matters," I laugh out the words.

"There are some things you don't need to know." I open my mouth to protest but then he interrupts, "until it becomes a problem."

"Do you need me to tell you that it was a problem the minute the Post got ahold of the story?" I say more calmly than I feel.

"I was..."

"Handling it," I finish for him. "*I* handled it." I flick my eyes to Evangeline, who is standing in the kitchen with a cup of coffee in hand and a worrisome expression.

Rausch stands up, motioning between the two of us. "So, you held a press conference without consulting me?"

"We decided it would be better to control the narrative before the Post article came out," I explain.

He holds up a paper in his hand. "Did you actually blame the health care system for creating prostitution?" he asks.

"No", she protests.

He scans the paper again. "Correction, the greed of the pharmaceutical companies."

"I didn't say that," she says.

"How about men and social constructs?" he adds.

She lets out a frustrated breath and grabs the paper from him.

"That's not what I meant," she protests. "They twisted my words."

"If you had come to me first, I would have helped you put together a statement they couldn't have twisted," he demands.

Evangeline tosses the paper onto the kitchen island with a slap. "I'm not going to lie to people. I just told my story."

She catches my eye and I hold it for several heartbeats, feeling the wave of emotion cross the room.

"Do you think people care about the truth?"

"Aren't journalists supposed to be unbiased?" she asks.

"That's a very naïve way of looking at things," he scoffs. "Do you know who owns the Post?" he asks but doesn't wait for an answer. "Look it up and you'll understand why I say that papers are a business. They care about profits. Spinning a story to be profitable is what they do. So, you can tell them your story about how you had to drop out of college to pay for your grandmother's care and they will tell the story about the Democrats move towards a socialist health care system!"

His voice echoes off the clay bricks of the fireplace and the room goes silent.

Shit.

I hate it when Rausch is right.

"They don't know how much work you've done for the foundation, for domestic abuse victims," Rausch says with slight indignation. "Or what you've given up in order to serve your community, or what a generous person you are." He looks like he could go on but doesn't.

"What can I do?" Evangeline steps forward, her back straight with a determined expression.

"Now that the cat's out of the bag, let them see who you are," he explains.

"What does that mean exactly?" I ask with trepidation.

"More press coverage, speaking engagements, public appearances with the two of you together," Rausch rattles off.

"I was thinking more behind the scenes." She slumps against the arm of the couch.

"There's no going back now," Rausch warns.

"Darren's running, not me."

"Do you know the saying, behind every powerful man is an even more powerful woman?" Rausch cracks a rare smile.

Evangeline wags her finger in front of him. "Do not try to flatter me in order to get what you want." She makes her way into the kitchen and scoops up her coffee mug.

Rausch follows her and I watch in amusement. "Obama was lagging in the polls until Michelle started campaigning for him."

Evangeline peers at him over the lip of her mug with narrowed eyes.

"Who do you think was running the country, Bill or Hillary?" Rausch continues and I have to cough into my fist so I don't laugh out loud.

She sets the cup down and places a hand on her hip, shaking her head.

"It's not gonna work."

"Do you think Jack would have been elected without Jackie?"

"Oh my God! Darren," she waves a hand at me. "Help me out here. I just can't with him today," she says, and dumps the remaining coffee into the sink.

"I thought it was a pretty good one," I laugh.

"Do not agree with him," she pleads.

Rausch stands with his hands clasped in front of him and a straight face.

"What about all the negative press?" She waves a hand.

"Langley has nothing now. Everything's out in the open," I say, peering over at Rausch. "Right?"

A fleeting thought about the letter my mother wrote, and I can't help but think there are other skeletons hidden in my family's closet.

He clears his throat. "Give it a week, and the press will have moved on," he explains. "And don't go rogue anymore. I can coach you."

Evangeline looks to me for confirmation.

"We can't hide out here for the rest of the campaign, and Rausch is right, things will blow over."

A wry smile plays at the corners of her lips, and I roll my eyes.

"You heard that too," Rausch says to her, raising an eyebrow, but the rest of his face remains impassive. "Darren said I was right."

"Don't let it go to your head." I laugh, and my phone vibrates.

Evangeline picks it up to hand it to me. I can see the worry in her eyes, but I shake my head to convey that now's not the time to discuss. Not with Rausch here. She hands it to me, and I shove it in my pocket.

"I need to get back to Washington. I'll put together some

appearances and speaking engagements," he says, pointing at Evangeline, who still doesn't look pleased.

As soon as the door shuts, she turns to me. "You've been speaking to your grandfather? When were you going to tell me?" She folds her arms over her chest.

"I haven't been speaking to him," I reply truthfully and walk back into the kitchen. "He got my number, and he wants to meet."

She leans against the island. All she has to do is look at me to pull truths.

"With everything going on I never got a chance to tell you," I explain, opening the refrigerator and leaning inside but not finding anything I want.

"Are you going to see him?"

"I haven't decided yet." I slam the refrigerator door closed.

"What changed?" she asks.

"I wanted to meet him because I felt like I didn't know who my dad was."

"And you thought he'd be able to give that to you?" She circles her arms around me.

"Not really no, but at the time I thought he was the only family I had left." I kiss the tip of her nose and the top of her cheek. "I was wrong." I kiss her lips, tasting coffee and vanilla. "You're my family."

"You make it hard for me to leave," she says.

I pull back to look at her with a raised eyebrow.

"There's a board meeting for the foundation," she tells me, but she doesn't look excited. "This is the first time I'll see them after the press conference."

"You shouldn't worry about what they think of you," I tell her.

"I'm not, but I never got a chance to talk to Bethany or Audrina before." She shakes her head. "I blindsided them."

"They'll understand," I reassure her.

"I hope you're right. I don't want any of this to impact the foundation."

22

Boss's Orders

Evangeline

"*T*he shit has hit the fan now!"

"That's a little dramatic, don't you think?" I question.

"You were all over the news," Cleo says. "You're famous. I'm talking to a famous person right now."

"I haven't looked," I admit. "And I am *not* famous."

"What do you mean you haven't looked? Not even a peek, a Google search of your name?" she asks, shocked.

"It's just best I don't know what they're saying. Angie's been filtering through the news and only relaying anything on a need-to-know basis," I explain.

"Angie? The one that was after your husband?" I can almost see the roll of her eyes and the purse of her lips as she says it.

"She wasn't after…" I pinch my forehead. "Ok, that would be the one,"

"Hmm," she says judgmentally into the phone. "You can't trust a woman who flirts with a married man."

I bark out a laugh, regretting that I even confided in her about it.

"What?"

"We literally slept with other women's husbands for a living," I point out with a hint of humor. "Are you saying I shouldn't trust you?"

"That's different. We got paid for it," she reasons. "And you're a respectable wife of a politician now."

"I don't know about respectable. Not after that press conference," I shake my head and then there's silence on the other line.

"Evan, you're the best person I know."

"Well, tell that to the ladies on the board," I say as we pull up in front of the office building.

"If they don't know that already, hun, then they don't know you at all," Cleo confirms.

"I gotta go." I smile and hang up the phone just as Bailey parks the car.

He opens the door for me and then starts to follow me inside. "I don't need a bodyguard, or whatever this is," I tell him with an annoyed tone.

"Boss's orders," Bailey explains, holding the door open for me.

"Do you always do what Darren says?"

"If I wanna keep my job," he says with all seriousness.

"I just don't think it's necessary," I huff, punching the button for the elevator. "I'm not the one running for office."

"Mr. Walker thinks it is." Bailey stands behind me in the elevator, his arms crossed over his chest.

"Do people really hate me that much?" I ask with a slight laugh, but inside I'm anything but laughing. Darren and I agreed not to look at the news or social media. It's better for my mental health, but if Darren insists on Bailey coming with me then I'm assuming things are not good. With the election several months away, I can only hope I haven't done irreparable damage.

I give Bailey a look that says he's not welcome inside, so he concedes and stands outside the door while I enter the boardroom.

The chatter in the room dies down to a whisper. I get excited when I see Rebecca at the back of the room, but she resumes her conversation with one of the other members. The only friendly face is Bethany's as she gives me a sympathetic smile. I take a seat next to her and set my purse on the table.

"I didn't have time to tell you beforehand or I would have," I explain. "I hope this isn't an issue for the foundation."

"Some of the funding has already been pulled," she explains, and my face falls.

"I wasn't prepared for how it would impact the charity," I admit. "I'm sorry. I hope this doesn't ruin the charity gala we have planned."

"It's still a few weeks off so I wouldn't worry. Reporters have been calling to get a statement," she replies.

"Oh," is all I can muster.

Bethany notices me looking at Rebecca. She stands, pulling me with her outside the room.

Bailey steps aside and Bethany looks at him, startled.

"Have you received threats?" She walks across the hall to a breakroom—Bailey close behind.

"Darren thought it would be wise."

She grabs two cups, fills them with coffee and hands one to me. Leaning against the counter she looks at me thoughtfully.

"I watched the press conference," she states, and I look at her with a weary expression. I can only imagine what she thinks of me. "So that's how you and Darren really met. Sounds like Darren," she laughs and then looks at me thoughtfully. "He's really turned things around and no doubt it's because of you."

"I really am sorry about the funding. I had no idea," I apologize.

Bethany lets out a breath. "If those donors can't be sympathetic then they don't understand the mission of the Abigail Pershing Foundation."

I smile, holding the cup of coffee in my hand, "I'm glad to know you feel that way."

"I'm very impressed with how far you've come. I was very close with my grandmother too," she adds. "The way you talked about her was very moving. She must have been very proud of you."

"She didn't know I paid for her care with the money I earned as an escort. She thought I had a journalism degree and was working for a paper."

"I was talking about how proud she must have been of your character. You have a big heart and a lot of drive, especially for someone so young. It's too bad she won't be here to witness who you will become," Bethany explains, placing a gentle hand on my arm and giving it a motherly squeeze.

"I just did what I had to do."

"Don't ever downplay the hard choices you've had to make. It's made you who you are," Bethany says.

"I haven't had a chance to talk to Audrina," I say.

"I don't think you have anything to worry about." She gives me a wink. "Audrina might be a tough cookie, but she has a soft spot for Darren. If you make him happy, that's all that matters."

We go back into the conference room, and I call the meeting to order. The agenda is light since the venue has been booked but there are still a few spots open for auction items.

"I was thinking we need something really big to draw in a lot of money," I ponder out loud.

"What about an experience?" Rebecca looks tired, as if she'd forgotten to put on makeup.

"I like that idea. We just need to come up with some places or people to contact," I offer.

"What if we appeal to the parents who want their kids to get into a good college?" Bethany interjects and I tilt my head at her, interested. "College coaches cost a lot of money. If we knew someone who'd be willing to offer that as a donation…" she trails off.

"That's promising," I smile.

"What about Darren? He went to Georgetown. He's a legacy. Surely, he has some advice to impart?" Bethany inquires, a hopeful expression on her face.

"Oh, I can ask him," I reply.

Bethany laughs. "You could voluntell him."

It takes me a minute to get her meaning and smile. I write that down on the list but that gets me thinking.

"What if we get someone famous to offer a lunch date?" I propose.

"Who?"

With all the partying Alistair does, I wonder if he knows anyone. "I'll ask around, figure something out." I make a note to reach out to Alistair.

"You *are* resourceful," she says, and I'm not sure if it's a friendly comment or not. I shake it off hoping that when the meeting is over, I'll get a chance to talk to her.

"Ok well, if we don't have any other business, we'll touch base in a couple weeks to finalize everything," I close out the meeting and start packing up my things.

"Seriously, Darren would be great. He could even offer some kind of coaching for the Bar exam," Bethany exclaims as she hoists her bag up her shoulder.

I feel bad because I'm not paying attention. I look in Rebecca's direction so I can catch her before she leaves, but she's already gone.

23

Gregory Allen Walker

Darren

*A*wkwardly, I sit in the diner, playing with the edges of the menu while I eye the door every time someone comes in. I lift my wrist and check the time again.

"Can I get you some more coffee?" the waitress asks.

"No." I throw a couple bills down and head for the exit.

My grandfather, Gregory Allen Walker, is standing in the parking lot. He's tall and lanky like my father, with gray hair peeking out of a ball cap. I don't wait for him to say anything and walk past him to my car.

"Darren, please!" he calls after me.

"You know, *I* didn't even know if I wanted to meet *you*," I say angrily. "And you stood *me* up."

"I'm here," he says. "I've been standing out here since you walked in," he pulls the ball cap off and scratches his head.

"This isn't what I need right now," I grumble and start to walk away again.

"I was nervous," he explains. "Didn't know how to talk to you after all these years."

"How about explaining why?"

"That's not an easy answer," he says.

"Okay, well let's start with why you were arrested for arson?" I ask angrily.

His eyes grow wide.

"Did you do a background check on me or something?" he scoffs and then comes to the conclusion. "Rausch," he laughs and shakes his head.

"You know him?" I can't hide the shock from creeping into my voice. Of course he knows him.

"You could say that."

"I didn't come here for more riddles."

"Then why did you come?" He shakes his head.

"I want to know why my father didn't want you in his life."

He looks at me sadly, deep regret lining his face and in his dark blue eyes.

"Can we sit down and talk?" he asks, motioning to the diner.

When we enter, the waitress recognizes him. "Hey there Allen, you want your usual?"

"No, just some coffee." Then he smiles real big. "This is my grandson."

She points her pen at me. "I thought you looked familiar. Aren't you running for congress?"

"That would be me." I offer a small smile.

"My daughter couldn't stop watching those ads." She gives me a wink.

I try my best to give her a smile. "Just coffee for me, too."

We take a seat in the booth at the far back where it's not so crowded.

"So?" he sits across from me, and it's a bit jarring how much he reminds me of my father—same nose, same eye color, same deep thoughtful brow.

The waitress pours our coffees and I hold on to the cup.

"Why did my father hate you?" I ask bluntly.

He pours a container of half and half into the cup and stirs it with the spoon before clearing his throat. "Was he a good father to you?" he surprises me by asking.

It takes me a moment to answer, not because I need to contemplate but because I'm wondering why he's asking.

"Yes."

"Good. That's good," he nods, still staring down at the coffee and cream swirling together.

"You didn't answer my question."

"Because I wasn't." He pauses, looking up at me. "I wasn't a good father."

"Why?"

He sits back in the booth and looks out the window. "I wasn't around a lot and when I was, I drank too much," he shrugs.

"That's not something you disown a parent for," I speculate.

"All that's in the past. My son is gone," he says sadly.

"That's why you showed up at the funeral, to say good-bye?" I ask.

"A father has a right to be there when his son is put in the ground," he says, jabbing a finger into the table. "No matter what happened."

I can understand his anger but there are still so many questions.

"What about his brothers?" I shake my head. "They didn't come."

"Your father didn't want anything to do with his family. I came to tell him when his brother Colt died, but he was still so angry—." He pauses. "Well, it doesn't matter now."

"That's when I saw you at the house," I say.

"You remember that?" He smiles. "You were a little kid. Must have been around eight or so."

"I was ten."

"I never got a chance to know you," he explains.

135

"You could have contacted me when I was in college, but you waited until my father died."

"I just figured I'd let things be. When I heard he died in that helicopter accident…" He trails off, holding the mug in his shaky hands and taking a sip.

I sit back in the booth, turning the cup around in my hand, trying to make sense of it. I can't shake the feeling that it's more than just my grandfather being a drunk.

"Why did you set that house on fire?" I inquire.

"What does it matter now?"

"Because it does. Is that why my father hated you? Whose house was it?" I slam my fist on the table, causing the coffee mugs to shake.

"I thought he was taking advantage of my son!" A few people turn to look at us. "I saw them together." He casts his eyes to the ceiling as if he's trying to make an apology but all I can see is anger lining his face. "I was drunk, and I was mad, and I made a mistake that I paid for."

There's a silence between us that could swallow me whole. If I understand him correctly, I'm horrified. He must see the expression on my face.

"I'm not the same person I was back then."

"I don't understand. Saw who together?" I shake my head, thinking this can't be right, I'm mistaken.

"A neighbor boy. I saw them kissing before they went into the basement. I thought—" He shakes his head as if trying to stop the memory from coming. "I had a bottle of Jack and a lighter."

I close my eyes and rub my forehead. He loved my mother. I saw it. I saw the way he took care of her, the way he would lead her into a room, the look of admiration and love in his eyes. I couldn't have imagined all that.

"He left for college and never looked back at where he came from. I thought when he married your mother, he put all that behind him. We could forget the past and move on, but he was just living a lie," he explains, and I feel like my world just dropped right out from under me.

"What are you saying?" I manage to get out.

"You wanted to know why we didn't speak, why I never got to be in your life? It's because I couldn't accept him." He throws his hands in the air.

The diner spins, and I grip the table to get my bearings while he continues.

"Then Dexter comes back, says he forgives me for setting his house on fire and that he's in love with my son and has been for years. That I should love him for who he is, but how can I do that?" He challenges. "How can I do that when I didn't even know who he was?"

"Dexter?"

"Dexter Rausch," he confirms, and my world tilts. I feel sick, like I could vomit right here. I have to take a sip of water and count my breaths.

"I know what you think of me. I wasn't a good person. When I tried to make it right, he didn't want anything to do with me. Dexter comes back, offers me money to keep quiet like I was a liability instead of a father," he fumes.

"I have to leave." I stand up and rush out of the diner.

My grandfather calls after me. "I warned you. No good can come of opening up the past," he yells as if there's a winning side in all this. "I'm sorry," he offers.

"You're sorry." I laugh. "You drop a bomb like that, and you say you're sorry?"

I run a hand over my face as if that will clear my head.

"How can I believe you? How can I know you're not doing this to get back at me or my father?" I demand.

"You know I'm telling the truth. You know because you saw it just like I did, but you didn't want to believe it."

I want to punch him. I want to punch him because he's right.

"No wonder my father didn't want anything to do with

137

you," I spit, pacing in front of him, kicking up the stone of the gravel parking lot.

"Darren," he pleads. "I know I'm on the wrong side of whatever line," he tries to explain, shaking his head. "Do you think I wanted my son in the ground thinking that I wasn't proud of him?" he questions.

"You wanted to have a relationship with me, and—Jesus," I run my hand through my hair. "This was a hell of a way to start."

I stalk to my car and peel out of the parking lot.

I start to pick out events, gestures, looks, that I thought were innocent that now start to take on a whole new perspective.

The letter. The fucking letter.

24

Smart Girl

Evangeline

"Here's a list of the speaking engagements," Angie hands me a piece of paper and I skim down the list.

There are rotary clubs, Women's Chamber of Commerce, and then I see the last organization on the list.

"The Daughters of the American Revolution?" I shake my head. "They sound Republican."

"They're not a political organization," Angie explains. "They're actually a charity heavily involved in preserving America's history and patriotism through children's education."

"What are the talking points?" I catch Darren's eye as he passes by, and he doesn't look happy.

"Just steer clear of mentioning anything pro-choice or gun control and you'll be fine," Angie interrupts.

I scrunch up my nose. "You said they're not Republicans?" I joke while making a note on my paper.

Angie doesn't miss a beat and I'm sure it's because she's

used to my sarcasm by now. "Make sure to talk about Dare's commitment to education and his plans to get more government grants. That should go over really well," she instructs, and the way she calls him Dare, just grates on my nerves.

"Sounds easier said than done," I explain, trying to focus.

"Do you need me to write up a speech?" she looks up from her computer. "I was quite good on the debate team."

"I'm sure you were."

"I hated my public speaking classes in college, but the more I did it the easier it got."

"I can relate, but unfortunately, I never got to the part where it got easier."

"Oh well, you did really well at the press conference."

I purse my lips trying not to take offense to that when I hear a bang come from Darren's office.

"I should probably check on him," Angie tries to stand but I stop her.

"I'm sure he's fine."

"Well, you don't know Dare. When he gets in a mood, we all end up paying for it," she explains, and I blanch.

"I don't know my own husband?"

"Oh my gosh, no! I just meant at work. That's all." She brushes me off. "You're lucky, you don't have to worry about any of that now," she says flippantly.

"What do you mean?"

"I meant that you don't have to worry about working," she offers.

"Oh, I see what you're saying." I tap the pen to my lips. "Since I'm *married* to Darren," I finish for her. "Well, you should remember that." I narrow my eyes at her.

"I'm sorry, that's not—" she starts to say but I interrupt her.

"I'm sure you're a smart girl or *Darren* wouldn't have hired you and Rausch wouldn't put up with you, but someone with your education should know better than to flirt with a married man," I say coolly. "Especially one that's running for congress."

"Evan," she gives a nervous laugh as if she thinks I'm joking. "I don't know what you think…"

"It's Mrs. Walker, and I think you're embarrassing yourself."

"You have the wrong idea. Darren and I just work really well together. There's nothing going on," she explains with a bit of arrogance.

"Oh, I know there's nothing going on." I can't help but let out a small condescending laugh. "Working to help get Darren elected is a privilege, one that you shouldn't take advantage of. And if you really want Darren to win, then you should remember that."

She closes her mouth and at least I see remorse on her face.

"Do we understand each other?"

"Yes, Mrs. Walker," she says.

A commotion in the office gets my attention and it looks as though there's a gathering outside the office.

I grab Ethel as she passes by. "What's going on?"

"The campaign ad started running during prime time," she says with a giddy smile. "Right between Jeopardy and America's Funniest Home Videos," she adds.

"I'm not tracking," I say. "What's with the gawkers?"

One of the volunteers cues up the ad on the tv screen. Darren appears in frame, his hair messy from the wind and his shirt collar unbuttoned, sans tie. He doesn't look like a politician as he strides down the street talking about his commitment and belief in the community. When he smiles into the camera at the end, I begin to understand.

"What in the hell?" Rausch pushes through the crowd, straightening his tie as if he'd just been accosted by a mob. "What are all these women doing on the street?"

"Well, they ain't here for you," Ethel says with a hand on her hip, raising her eyebrow.

Rausch ignores her and then looks up at the tv screen. "Is that the ad?" He squints and then his eyes go wide. Before I can say anything, he yells, "Darren, Jesus Christ!"

"I like the ad," I say, shrugging. "And it looks like half the town's single women do too," I giggle. "Oh, and a few married ones too." I laugh.

"You bellowed?" Darren appears with a scowl on his face.

"What the hell is that?" Rausch motions to the tv screen.

"That there is what you call a thirst trap," Ethel answers for him.

Rausch just blinks at her.

"Do you need me to explain what a…" Ethel starts to say.

"I know what a… Jesus, is this a frat house or a campaign office?" Rausch asks.

"You don't like it?" Darren inquires with a bit of the old playboy attitude he used to have.

"It looks more like you're selling cologne than a political advertisement."

"See, thirst trap," Ethel interjects.

"Don't you have things to do?"

Ethel raises an eyebrow and gives me a smile.

"Then you should have *been* here, but you bailed on me," Darren interjects, his voice sounding more clipped than usual.

Darren studies him like he's trying to decipher something in the lines in his face. Rausch looks back at him, annoyed, but then his expression changes and the air between them becomes thick. I touch Darren's arm.

"The ad felt stiff," Darren finally says, his words cutting across the space between them.

"He was walking like he had a stick up his ass." Ethel pipes up and Darren shakes his head at her.

"What I mean is that the voters aren't going to respond to someone…"

"Who has a stick up their ass?" Ethel asks, feigning innocence.

"Ethel," he warns.

"I know when I'm not wanted." And Ethel walks back over to her desk.

Before Rausch can respond, Darren's gone.

Rausch clears his throat and then gestures to the window. "Do something about that." I grab my purse from Angie's desk and run after Darren. I don't get very far down the block when I bump into someone exiting one of the stores.

"So sorry," I exclaim, grabbing onto her arm to steady her.

"You're Evangeline Walker," she says, surprised as she looks me up and down. She's a young woman, probably only a few years older than me, with brown hair pulled back with a clip.

"Yes," I answer cautiously.

"I've been meaning to come see you, but it's been so busy here." She locks up the door behind her. "My mom owns the shop but she's been in the hospital, so I've taken over."

"Oh, I'm so sorry."

"It's not serious. I wanted to thank you," she surprises me by saying.

I shake my head in confusion.

"Ethan from Rustic Charm Designs said you wanted to buy local. He's been in a few times." She motions to her shop.

"And Henry said you had donated some stuff to his place." She hooks her thumb down the block where Henry's Hand Me Downs is.

"I'm so glad," I exclaim. "But I can't take credit for that. Admittedly, I've been so busy with everything," I motion to the campaign office. "That I've let Ethan run the show," I laugh nervously.

"It means a lot to the town," she says with sincerity. "And I just wanted to say how much I admire you."

To say I'm taken aback is an understatement.

"I watched the press conference and that took real courage." She reaches out to take my hand. "I'm Maddie, by the way," she introduces herself.

"It's so nice to meet you," I shake her hand.

"I know some folks in town might be a bit *old fashioned*, but what you said about taking care of your grandmother, it just hit home, especially with my mom's surgery. It's so expensive and I know it's not the same thing, but I'd do anything for her, ya know?" She smiles. "Well, anyway, I'm happy I ran into you," she remarks. "If you have any signs I can place in the window I'd be happy to. I know Henry would, too, and a few of the other shop owners."

"That'd be wonderful. Thank you." My phone vibrates in my pocket, and I hold up a finger for her to wait.

"Yes, can you hold on one minute?" I ask, and then hold my hand over the phone.

"The office is still open. If you want to head on in and ask for Ethel, she'll give you some signs," I offer.

"Will do, so nice to meet you," Maddie smiles and then heads over to the campaign office.

"I'm back, sorry about that," I apologize.

"Hello, this is Lucy, I represent Finn McCarthy. I advised Finn not to do the charity," she says and my heart sinks.

"I'm sorry to hear that."

"Yes, well, Finn rarely listens to me anyway, which is why he gets himself into trouble. His reputation could use an overhaul, I just didn't think this particular charity was going to accomplish that, considering..." she leaves the sentence hanging.

"Yes well, the Abigail Pershing Foundation helps battered women, and the money from the auction would help us open another safe house," I try to explain.

"I know all of that already, but it's not always about the charity itself but the people who run it."

"I see." I can't help the disappointment in my voice.

"Finn will be in New York that weekend for some press, and he'd like to attend the charity personally," she explains.

"Well, that's wonderful. I can email you the details and send a ticket for him."

"Excellent, have a good day." And the phone goes dead.

25

Phallic Monuments

Darren

"*D*arren, help me with this," Evangeline calls frantically from the bedroom, holding a long pearl necklace in her hand. "I can't get the clasp," she explains as soon as I enter the bedroom.

"Where did you get these?" I ask, admiring the necklace in my hands.

"I bought them, instead of a car," she teases, and I smile.

She holds her hair out of the way as I lay the necklace against her chest and then work the clasp at the back clumsily. I watch as she waits nervously for me to finish, checking the time on her phone every few seconds.

"My fingers are too big. Hang on, I think I've got it," I reassure as the necklace falls into place and the long single strand sways down her bare back. I can't help but run my knuckles down her spine as I look at her in the mirror. She meets my gaze and holds it for a second.

I open my mouth but what comes out is, "This is quite a dress," instead of what I want to say. I place a kiss on her bare shoulder, admiring the way the back of her dress is open and barely covers the top of her tailbone. She looks elegant and confident, fitting into her role better than I have ever imagined.

She grabs her gloves from the back of the chair. "We're going to be late." She rushes out of the room and down the stairs. I follow dutifully. Bailey waits at the curb with the sedan, and we duck inside.

It's early evening, and as we get closer to the National Mall, the color of the sky deepens to a midnight blue, the buildings lighting up. She crosses her legs, looking out the window, and she shakes her foot with a nervous fervor.

I place my hand on her thigh. "Everything's going to be fine," I reassure her.

"It's the first event I've put on as chairwoman and I want it to be perfect."

"You don't have anything to prove." I give her leg a squeeze.

"Of course I do!" she says with exasperation. "Have you seen the sky? The weather wasn't calling for rain and yet"—she tosses a hand towards the window—"it very much looks like rain."

"Is this an outdoor event?"

"It's on the rooftop terrace."

"Certainly, you have a contingency plan."

"Of course, Darren, but the point of having it on the terrace is the view of the National Mall." As if this should be obvious.

"And the National Mall will convince people to donate?"

"Don't be a smartass." She playfully smacks my arm. "It can't help but inspire people to dig a little deeper into their pockets, right? That's what I was going for anyway."

"You're very cute when you're nervous." I hold onto her chin.

"I'm glad you think so because when I'm nervous I have to pee, and this dress is not conducive to peeing," she sighs.

"Relax," I find the slit in her dress and run my hand along her bare leg, causing goosebumps to form in my wake. Her reaction to my touch is always a turn on.

She sighs heavily but places her hand on top of mine, stopping my progress before I reach the edge of her panties. "This dress is also not conducive to car sex," she explains, causing me to pout. "Besides, we're here."

I look out the window as we pull along the circular drive of the National Museum of American History, a large rectangular stone building with a flat roof. The stone front is lit up and welcoming.

The rooftop has a perfect view of the Washington Monument, which glows like a beacon in the distance. I shove my hands in my pockets as I look out over the National Mall, and it's not the rich history that distracts me, but rather the conversation with my grandfather that I can't seem to pause in my head.

Evangeline gives me a peck on the cheek, and I give her a weak smile back. "Sorry, I'll be back. I have to check on the auction and make sure the food is here," she apologizes, and I give her a weak smile.

"Is everything okay?" she asks. Her hand lingers on my arm.

"Go, go. I won't get into too much trouble," I tease, and she gives me a warning glance before she heads in the direction of Bethany, who seems to have just arrived. The two of them link arms and rush off.

I turn back to the Washington Monument, admiring the towering obelisk that was built to honor George Washington after the Revolutionary War, and is still the tallest man-made masonry structure to this day. A waiter glides by with a tray of champagne, and I manage to snatch one before he disappears as the space begins to fill up with Washington's fattest wallets. I smile as I watch impressed faces admiring flower arrangements and place settings, details that escaped me until now.

My wife did all this. I reach out and touch the pale blue linen draped over a nearby table. It's not just the linen or the flowers, or even the champagne—it's the care and the foresight into putting together an event that will no doubt change people's lives for the better.

"Have you ever wondered if the other founding fathers made Washington's monument look like a giant dick because they were jealous of his popularity?" Alistair ruins my thoughts as he appears out of nowhere.

"For one, the founding fathers didn't design the monument and no, I have never thought about whether it was designed to look phallic as a fuck you."

Alistair quirks his mouth and I turn back to the monument that is now looking more phallic by the minute thanks to him.

"Your sister's not here with you, is she?" I ask.

"Oh God no," he replies. "She's been evading my parents lately because they've been trying to marry her off to some prince in Belgium." He waves his hand.

"That's... so far away," I observe.

"I think that's the point," Alistair asserts, raising an eyebrow and then resting his elbows casually on the table.

"Please tell me you have Macallan." He bats his eyes at the bartender as if this will magically produce what he wants.

She eyes him wearily and produces two glasses of amber liquid. Alistair takes a sip and makes a disgruntled face. "So that's a no," he says.

"It's a charity function, what did you expect?" I take a healthy sip of my drink until I've finished the whole glass.

I order another. Alistair refuses.

"Caroline and Remington have been on a tear," Alistair complains, but I tune him out as I watch Evangeline work the room. Her back is to me while she talks animatedly to a group, the string of pearls swaying down her bare back.

I finish off the drink and pull at the collar of my shirt, loosening the bowtie just enough to breathe freely. Not just because she's the most beautiful woman in the room; it's how she manages to captivate everyone in her presence—as if she's always belonged.

I used to think that was a bad thing, getting comfortable in this life with its pretentious chokehold on anyone within the circle, but not anymore. It's not this life that has a chokehold on me, it's her.

"And Remington invites my boss over for dinner as if that's normal," Alistair continues, and I shake my head.

"Excuse me," I apologize and hear him call after me as I make my way over to Evangeline.

When I approach, I place my hand on the small of her back, and then discreetly wrap the strand of pearls around my fist, feeling the familiar pull in my stomach.

She sucks in a breath, and I can feel the goosebumps form on her back.

I'm incorrigible, thinking of fucking my wife while she shmoozes with Catharina Hale, an heiress by marriage and a known philanthropist, but I can't help it.

"I was very impressed with your story," I overhear her say to Evangeline. "I'd love to take a tour of Compton House when the renovations are complete," Catharina says.

"Sorry to interrupt," I apologize.

"Darren," Catharina says, extending her hand for me to take.

Reluctantly, I let go of the pearls to shake her hand. "Nice to see you again," I reply.

"We're hoping to have the renovations completed before the end of the year and start taking in more women and children. Capacity will be increased by at least ten more units," Evangeline explains with pride.

"Impressive," Catharina acknowledges.

"I've been thinking of doing the same thing with a property I own in Arizona," Evangeline announces.

"Oh?" This is the first I've heard of it, but we've had little time for conversations lately.

"Yes," Evangeline continues. "I inherited my grandparents' home"—she tilts her head ever so slightly in my direction with a smile—"and I'd love to do something useful with it."

"I think that's a wonderful idea. If you're able to pull off an event like this, then there's no telling what else you could do," Catharina compliments.

"Well, the planning committee put this together. There is a group of wonderful volunteers that did all this." Evangeline gestures around to the terrace that is filled with elegantly decorated tables, flowers, and bistro lights that glow like fireflies in the ever-darkening night.

"I'd love to learn more. Perhaps we can meet sometime next week?" Catharina requests. "I'll be in touch."

She waves to someone in the distance and excuses herself. Evangeline turns to me with a girlish smile on her face.

"When did you decide what you wanted to do with the house?"

"Just now," she explains. "I mean, I've been thinking about it since I saw all the work that was being done to Compton House, and it got me thinking. The Mirabella Mitchell House has a really nice ring to it—Mirabella House for short."

"After your grandmother," I smile and tug her closer to me so I can kiss her temple. "I think that's a wonderful idea."

"Me too," she frowns. "Have you been drinking?"

"It's a party." Her smile returns but only slightly. "If I haven't told you how proud I am of you, just know that I am. This is,"—I pause—"very impressive."

Evangeline looks over my shoulder and I track her gaze to

see Rebecca Langley moving through the crowd, but thankfully I don't see her husband with her.

"I need to," she starts to say, about to follow her, but then a group of women walk towards us preventing her from leaving.

"Thank you so much for inviting us," one of the women says. She looks at Evangeline's dress and then around the room. "Are you sure we should be here though? I just can't help feeling like we don't really fit in."

Evangeline takes her hand. "You helped bring this event to life. If anything, you belong here more than anyone. I want you to enjoy the evening and don't ever think you don't belong because *I* want you here."

"Thank you," the woman says, "for everything." Their attention is diverted as they spot one of the more popular attendees of the night, an Irish actor.

I hook my thumb in his direction. "Finn McCarthy?" I raise an eyebrow. "Didn't he star in and direct that movie?" I inquire, suddenly interested.

"I think so, yeah. I didn't know you liked romance movies."

"I have a variety of tastes," I answer, feeling a bit unsteady on my feet. Admittedly, I shouldn't have downed both glasses in quick succession.

"Didn't have anything to do with it being R rated, about an older woman and a younger man?"

"It was done very artistically. And older women are more Alistair's style." I wink.

"You went together to see it, didn't you?"

"No, that would be weird. We rented it, like self-respecting pervs," I say pointedly.

"Darren, are you sure you're okay? You've been off lately." She gives me a look of concern.

"I'm fine," I lie.

She eyes me critically as if she can see right through my bullshit, but right now is not the time.

"So, those were the volunteers?" I change the subject.

"Yes, and they're residents of Compton House. Organizing an event this size is something they can put on their resume."

"You continue to surprise me," I entreat.

"Good surprise?" she asks, lifting an eyebrow.

I nod, leaning down to kiss her.

"Speaking of surprises," she says, and I'm getting a hint of an ominous tone. "One of the auction prizes had to drop out, and I volunteered you."

"How can an auction prize drop out?" I ask curiously.

"Well, this year we're auctioning off people," she explains, and I quirk a skeptical eyebrow. "Like lunch with a famous actor."

"Ah, well, you'll have to explain to me how you wrangled Finn McCarthy into that," I say, although when Evangeline wants something, she somehow manages to get it.

"His public image needed an overhaul and being associated with a charity is the perfect way to do that. Not to mention his starting bid is a pretty penny," she gloats.

"Wait, you volunteered me?" I ask, skeptically.

"Yes, we're calling it 'drinks with a reformed playboy'," she laughs.

"You're not serious," I challenge.

She giggles and it sounds like a symphony of clinking glasses.

"Of course not. It's an hour of your time to help some lucky kid with rich parents to prep for the Bar exam," she explains. "I'm sorry I didn't tell you about it sooner but you were so busy and…"

"It's fine," I soothe. "But people will bid on this?" I raise an eyebrow. "What's my starting bid?" I inquire, and she starts to walk through the crowded room. "Less than Finn

McCarthy?" I follow, and she pinches her fingers together by way of measurement.

"I don't know why anyone would want to have lunch with a famous actor anyway," I say indignantly.

"Well, your ad was pretty popular… until Finn's movie came out," she trails off.

"He stole my thunder," I grumble.

We stop in front of a glass window that reflects a view of the city, but more importantly her, and God I am so enamored that I forget she is auctioning me off like a prized pig.

I tap the glass. "What's in here?" I inquire innocently as I plan a way to steal her away from the event so that I can have a few moments with her alone.

She smiles, and I imagine she's thinking about last year's charity event just as I am, where I fucked her in the coat check room.

"It's an equipment room for the sound system," she explains with a wicked glint in her eyes.

I let my hand drop down her back to the curve of her ass and she sighs into my ear. "The auction starts soon," she announces, and I groan.

"I can be quick, you know that." I lift my eyebrows.

"I don't think that's something to brag about."

"I like to call it being efficient." I laugh, and see the resolve in her eyes as she glances towards the one-way glass.

I see Rausch's reflection as he enters the gala, my smile fades to a glower. "You didn't tell me Rausch was attending."

"What's going on with the two of you?" she demands.

I don't want to ruin this night for her, so I say, "Nothing." But with Rausch in attendance, I don't know how long I can keep my tongue.

She forces me to look at her. "Why don't I believe you?"

I don't get a chance to answer her because Alistair barges between us, holding his phone to his chest. "Do you know how to negotiate a hostage situation?"

"What?"

"Penelope says she's being held hostage by some visiting Emir at Blair House,"

"Penelope?" Evangeline asks.

"My monster of a sister," Alistair explains with an eye roll.

"I didn't know you had a sister. You've never mentioned her," she says.

"I try not to," he grouses. "She's been away at boarding school and now she's back home getting kidnapped, no doubt to get attention."

"Um, that—that sounds serious," Evangeline frets, looking between us with wide eyes.

"Not likely. She exaggerates, but you know, just in case, I need you to negotiate her release if it's real." He looks pointedly at me.

"Why me?"

"You're in politics," he replies as if it should be obvious.

"I'm running for Congress. I'm not a hostage negotiator," I exclaim.

"Same thing," Alistair says, holding the phone out to me while I shake my head and back away.

"Take it," he demands with a whisper-shout through gritted teeth.

"I'm not talking to some Saudi Prince," I whisper-shout back, looking at the phone as if it's a live bomb.

"You two are clearly busy, and I need to get the auction started. I hope you get your sister back," she calls over her shoulder as she disappears into the crowd.

"You and your sister are cock-blockers!" I exclaim.

"Alistair!" I hear Penelope yell through the phone, and he presses it back to his ear. "You can blame Darren if you become a concubine," he barks angrily as he walks away from me.

26

Starting Bid

Evangeline

"**E**verything okay?" Bethany asks.

I fold my arms over my chest. "I'm worried about Darren," I reply. "I think the campaign is really taking a toll on him."

"And what about you?"

"Me?"

"Yes, how are you doing with everything?"

I let out a breath. "It's been a while since someone has asked me that."

"Forgive me for not asking sooner," she apologizes.

"No, I just meant I don't think I've had time to really think about how I've felt," I offer.

"It's a lot," she offers, giving my arm a tight squeeze.

"I've been thinking the worst in people for so long that I've grown to expect it," I explain. "But Catharina Hale just offered to have lunch with me next week, and Finn McCarthy has been nothing but generous, and it's just so—" I don't finish the sentence.

"Overwhelming?" Bethany finishes for me.

"Yes," I reply.

"When you just be yourself, that's what people admire the most. And the ones that don't... it is more about them than it is about you," she offers.

"The VIP bags are set up near the exit," Audrina announces as she reaches the auction table. Rebecca stands awkwardly next to her.

"Oh good, as soon as the auction ends, we can start handing them as people leave," Bethany smiles.

"Rebecca, I wonder if I can..."

"We should get the auction started," she announces.

I tap the microphone to make sure it's on and it makes a muffled noise through the speakers.

"If you have not registered for the auction, you should do so now and get your paddles because the auction will be starting soon," I say to the crowd.

"Welcome, and thank you for coming to the annual charity gala for the Abigail Pershing Foundation. My name is Evangeline Walker, and as chairwoman of the foundation, I would like to say that this year we have some exciting items for you to bid on." I stop as guests applaud and wait for it to die down before I continue.

"I would first like to thank all of the members of the committee for helping to put this event on." I wave my hand to the side of the stage where Audrina, Bethany, and Rebecca stand. "And a very special thank you to the women of Compton House for helping to set up the event tonight." I point to the back of the room where some of the volunteers are standing, shocked and pleased expressions on their faces.

"Now that that's out of the way, let's get the auction started!" I boom, and the crowd claps.

"Okay, get your paddles ready because this first item is sure to be a bigger hit than his last movie. A lunch date with Finn McCarthy!" The crowd grows excited as Finn steps up onstage. I hand him the mic momentarily and look out into the crowd. I find Darren near the back and try to catch his eye to make sure he knows he's up next, but he seems preoccupied with Rausch.

"Thank you," Finn greets into the mic. "I'm happy to be here for such a good cause."

He hands the mic back to me.

"Our starting bid is one thousand dollars," I barely get out when several paddles are raised into the air. "Fifteen hundred anyone?" I knew Finn would draw in quite a large sum but as the price goes up and up, I'm flabbergasted.

"Ten thousand dollars going once, going twice," I announce. "Number 907, Finn McCarthy is yours!"

Finn raises his eyebrows at me as a very happy elderly woman, dripping in diamonds, ambles forward to claim her prize.

I look through the crowd for Darren again, but he's not paying attention to me or the auction. His back is to me, and he seems to be arguing with Rausch.

"Okay, our next auction item is a one-hour Bar Exam prep advice session with none other than my husband, Darren Walker—who's running for Congress, so if you're from District five, vote for Darren." I get a few laughs.

I thought my introduction would get his attention, but it hasn't. Rausch points in my direction and Darren smacks his hand away. I watch in horror as he gets in Rausch's face as if he's ready to brawl right here.

I look to Bethany for help, and she takes the mic from me while I step off the stage.

"Apologies, our next auction item will be a romantic meal for two cooked by Michelin chef Alain Ducasse," Bethany announces, and their attention is back to the stage instead of the scene unfolding in front of me.

Darren and Rausch are usually at each other's throats, but not like this. There's real anger on Darren's face as I step between them.

"Wanna tell me what the hell is going on?" I push against Darren's chest, his expression dropping as soon as he sees me.

Rausch adjusts his bowtie with an indignant look on his face. "I don't know *what* has gotten into you," he grumbles.

"God, do you always have to act like a pretentious prick?" Darren barks.

"I could ask the same about your petulant behavior," Rausch counters back.

"I would try to care what you think of me but that would take too much effort." Darren glares back at him while taking a sip of his drink.

"If that's the attitude you have no wonder you're sinking in the polls," Rausch reprimands.

"The only good thing about that is you drowning with me."

"Get your shit together."

"Darren," I bark out. "This isn't the place."

"You know what, Dexter?"

I've never heard him call Rausch by his first name.

"You can fuck off. You're fired," he announces as he stalks off.

I look back at Rausch in shock as he shakes his head, and then I follow Darren through the crowd, grabbing his arm and hauling him outside.

"What the fuck is going on, Darren?"

"Nothing," he heaves.

"Don't patronize me," I fume. "You know how much this night meant to me and you almost ruined the auction." I wave my hand towards the room, still able to hear Bethany as she manages the bidding.

"I'm sorry."

"You're sorry?" I pace in front of him. "You've been drinking, and then you pick a fight with Rausch."

"It's a party. Am I not allowed to enjoy a drink?"

"You've had more than just a drink. I haven't seen you like this since your parents…" I don't finish the sentence.

"Since my parents died? Are you serious?"

"Yes," I say quietly as I watch him imploding from the inside out. "What is going on, Darren?"

His hazel eyes are more green than brown at the moment. They settle on me.

"I met my grandfather," he tells me, and I remove my hand from him.

"When?" I question, surprised.

"I don't know," he runs a hand through his hair. "A few days ago, maybe a week," he offers.

"Why didn't you tell me?" I ask.

"You were busy with the gala, and I didn't want to…"

"That's bullshit, Darren," I bark, and that gets his attention. "Don't make excuses. What aren't you telling me?" I demand.

He narrows his eyes, holding onto the back of his neck while he paces in front of the door.

"You can talk to me," I coax him because I can see the turmoil in his eyes, and I want to take the burden from him.

"He told me the reason he was arrested was because he'd caught my father and a boy together. That he'd been confused and angry and drunk, and he'd set the house on fire," Darren explains, and his words steal my breath. The pearls at my neck suddenly feel tight.

"He thought your father and this boy were…" I start to say but I'm cut off.

"*Rausch* and my father," he starts to say, stopping in front of me. "The affair my father was having?" He pauses, and I search his eyes, my stomach tightening in response. "It was with Rausch."

"How do you even know your grandfather is telling you the truth?" I question. "You don't know if you can trust him, Darren." Right now, he's vulnerable. I know how that overwhelming need to have a connection to someone can lead you astray from what you know is right.

"You think *Rausch* would tell me the truth?" Darren counters. "It all makes sense now. That's what the letter was about. The third person in my parents' marriage was him."

I place my hand on his back. "Why didn't you tell me?"

"I didn't want to ruin this night for you." He pulls back to look at me, holding my face in his hands.

"Well, that went as planned," I say sarcastically.

"I'm sorry," he whispers into the crook of my neck. "I'm so sorry."

He ducks his head from me and looks back into the terrace. "I can't be in the same room as him."

I place my hands over his and search his eyes. I take Darren's hand. "I have to give closing remarks," I tell him.

"You should be enjoying your night and I ruined it. Exactly what I didn't want to happen," he apologizes.

"I'm your wife, Darren." I take hold of him. "Your burden is my burden. If you're hurting, then use me to take it away."

He stares at me, his eyes darkening and his lips parting. I swallow hard and take his hand as we rush through the hall as much as I can in my heels, avoiding the terrace and the guests.

27

Yes, Congressman

Darren

I can finally breath, but it does little to extinguish the anger that still burns hot inside of me at just the thought of Rausch. When he approached me earlier, acting as if he weren't harboring a huge secret, I couldn't hold it in any longer, seeing his smug face while he acted like he was my friend. I've never felt more betrayed in my life and everything I'd been holding in the past few days is now on the surface and I feel like I'm ready to implode.

Catharina Hale and her husband enjoy a glass of champagne only a few feet from me on the other side of the glass. I place my hand in front of them and wave ever so slightly to get their attention but nothing. They can't see me, but they can probably hear me if I called out loud enough or banged on the glass.

I turn and my gaze settles on my wife. The look of complete submission in her eyes has my stomach tightening and my cock stirring against the zipper of my slacks.

She slowly walks towards me, her heels clicking against

the tile, and the sound her dress makes as she moves, has me needy to rip it off. Standing before me, she's a wicked temptation with her blonde hair pulled back and her red lips parted ever so slightly. The thought of her red lipstick around my cock occupies every corner of my mind.

She pulls on my belt, freeing it from my waist and I touch the side of her face, softly caressing her cheek.

"On your knees," I command gruffly, and a wicked smile plays at the corners of her lips

"Yes," she obeys, kneeling down and looking up at me through her bangs.

"Yes what?"

She blinks innocently. She's beautiful and has me in knots and I'd do just about anything to have her. Even on her knees, she owns me. "Yes, Congressman."

I pull the button free and unzip my pants, my cock already hard and at attention. Wrapping my hand around the base I guide the head to her waiting lips while stroking her temple with the other.

She opens her mouth, the red lipstick glistening in the soft light, and her tongue darts out. When she wraps her mouth around my cock, I groan. As she wraps her lips around me, her blue eyes, like flames, peer up at me through her bangs and the sight of her almost makes me come.

I groan while fisting my cock and guide it in further until she takes all of me. On her knees and her mouth around my shaft is more than I can bear. I restrain myself from grabbing the back of her head and pumping into her mouth, but I don't know how long I can last.

I close my eyes and it's almost worse as the orgasm threatens to overtake me. Especially when her tongue swirls against me, causing my head to swell even more.

"Fuck," I grit out as I stroke her face and feel her hand move from my waist to my ass as she greedily brings me closer to her.

I don't want to come, not yet but she feels so good gripping me in her palm while sucking me off. When the temptation becomes too much, I reach down and grab her chin, lifting her up to me. When I kiss her, I taste the salty precum on her tongue and I press her tightly against me, kissing her as if I will never get another chance.

I turn her around to face the party, resting my lips against the back of her neck as my cock strains at her backside. Pulling the strap of her dress down, I expose her breast and groan the moment I notice the tight pink bud of her nipple.

Reaching down, I lift her dress up, exposing her G-string, the delicate thread of lace weaving between the firmness of her cheeks. She parts her legs, allowing me access to her already wet cunt.

She tries to turn around to face me but I stop her by grabbing onto the strand of pearls, tugging just enough to get her attention. With my palm against her back, I push her forward towards the glass.

"Hands on the glass, Queenie," I command, and she does as she's told like a good wife while I relieve her of her panties. She steps out of them, while I run my hand along her calf.

I take a step back and admire my wife, her breast exposed, palms pressed to the glass, facing a party with gossipy socialites, and rich old men. Her legs shake and her breathing is labored and *God*, she is beautiful. My cock juts out from my pants and I stand behind her, reaching around to stroke her clit that pulses under my touch. She leans greedily into me.

"So wet," I breath against her neck.

"Darren," she whines, and I fist my cock knowing the minute I'm inside her I won't be able to stop. "Please."

I slide into her and let out a desperate groan, pressing her further until her breast and cheek are crushed into the glass, her breath leaving an imprint.

She moans and gasps for air as I fuck into her at a

desperate pace. I wrap the pearls around my palm and hold onto her.

A guest walks up to the glass mere inches from us, smoothing a stray piece of hair back into place unaware of the wicked things I'm doing to my wife right now. Evangeline's eyes grow wide, and she suppresses a moan as she looks behind at me while I thrust into her.

"Don't take your hands off that glass, Evan," I demand, and her palm goes flat, eyes hooded and she turns back to face the party.

Guests mill around nearby tables and even though they can't see us, there's something so naughty, so wrong, about fucking her this way. It's what I needed. *She's* what I needed.

"Fuck, you feel good," I growl feeling the pull in my stomach and my orgasm beginning to build like a living breathing thing inside of me.

"Oh God," she moans as I drag my finger through her wetness and rub at a pace that causes her to shake and shudder, unaware of how her orgasm affects me. I yank hard, breaking the strand, pearls explode into the air and hit the ground making it sound like pounding rain.

Her cunt grips my fingers, and her legs shake, threatening to give out beneath her. I'm desperate to taste it. I pull out and turn her around, kissing her lips and then her jaw and make my way down her neck to her breast, the pert nipple just begging for me to pull it between my teeth and suck hard. She gasps and pulls at my hair until I'm level to her cunt. I lift her dress and when I do, my stomach tightens all over again and my cock strains as I latch onto her like a starving man on a deserted island even though moments ago I was inside her.

I lift her leg over my shoulder and feel her hands in my hair, tugging and pulling on the strands while I fuck her with my tongue. She tastes sweet and I can't get enough until she starts to shake all over again and her whines become louder – more desperate, I lift her up against the glass and push inside her once more, and this time I don't hold back. I see the want all over her face, the unequivocable love she holds for me like a real and visceral thing. Her fingernails dig into my skin through my shirt, the tuxedo jacket long since discarded, and when her pussy pulses around me with the first wave of another orgasm, I'm gone – so gone for her that no one else compares or ever could.

My own orgasm crashes into me like a crushing wave and I hold onto her while I ride it out, feeling her teeth bite into my shoulder making me shudder. I lean against her, and with my heart pounding forcefully, I let out a satisfied laugh. Holding her face in my hands, I kiss her, long and hard as if I hadn't just fucked her.

"God, I love you," I rasp, resting my forehead against hers trying to catch my breath as I let her down.

"Do you know how much this cost?" she asks, holding what's left of the necklace.

"I'll buy you a hundred of them if you like, just so I can break them again," I answer, admiring my freshly fucked wife.

She touches my face and looks at me as if to make sure I'm alright even though she's the one that was fucked with the force that threatened to break the one-way glass. And I love her for that. I love her for giving me everything that I need even if I don't deserve it. Especially when I don't deserve it.

"What are we going to do with this mess?" she inquires, looking at all the loose pearls that litter the ground. "I can't possibly pick them all up."

"Leave them," I reply, shaking my head.

"We should go home," she says grabbing her purse and dropping what's left of the necklace inside. Her expression changes when she pulls out her phone.

"Don't read the news," I tell her, being overprotective and angry that I even have to do so.

"It's not the news," she explains, holding the phone for me to read a text notification.

Rebecca: Can you meet for lunch tomorrow?

28

Great Things
Evangeline

The trees lining the street rustle with the wind as I walk up to the busy café and notice Rebecca at a table outside enjoying the view of the Potomac. The weather is warm, and the scent of cherry blossoms is carried on the same breeze that roughens the water.

I gesture to my lunch date as the hostess leads me through the tables.

"Thank you for meeting me," Rebecca greets, gesturing to the chair opposite her.

"I have to say I was surprised to hear from you," I reply, taking a seat. "You've been avoiding me," I accuse, getting to the point.

"I'm sorry about that," she says sheepishly.

Our waitress approaches. "Can I start you off with something to drink?" she asks with a perky smile.

"I'll take a martini," Rebecca replies, handing her the menu.

So, I guess this is how it's going to go.

"I'll have the same," I respond and hand her my menu as well. I don't think I could eat anyway.

"I don't want to sit here and act like everything is okay. It's not," Rebecca responds.

"I can appreciate that," I nod. "I understand that you're mad finding out about my past at that press conference." I shake my head.

"I knew about you before the press conference."

"How long have you known?" I question.

The waitress drops off our drinks, but I can't take my eyes off Rebecca.

As soon as the waitress leaves, I ask, "*How* did you know?"

"I know a lot of things I wish I didn't," she admits.

She's not just talking about my confession.

"I know what kind of man my husband is," she admits.

"He was a client," I admit. "But I never slept with your husband."

She shakes her head and sighs, taking a large sip of her martini. "I'd really like to believe that, but that's not what this is about."

"I'm sorry, I don't understand."

"I know you don't understand how things are done in my world. You might be married to Darren, but you didn't grow up like this," she gestures around at the upscale café with baskets of flowers and gold-plated silverware.

"There are certain expectations and well, I didn't want to admit that I had married the wrong person," she explains. "Not that it would matter to my family anyway."

"I'm sorry."

"I don't need you to be sorry. I just need you to listen," she states.

I nod, picking up the martini and taking a healthy sip because I think I'm gonna need it.

"I just don't know how you could look me in the eye,

knowing what kind of man my husband is," she shakes her head, and I can't seem to read her. She's angry but I'm not sure if she's angry at me anymore.

"I never meant to hurt you," I explain. "I honestly only ever saw you as my friend."

"I did too," she replies and then sits back in her chair, crossing her legs. She looks at her lap and smoothes down her skirt.

"You know, generations before me have had to put up with infidelity," she smiles sadly. "I guess I always expected it."

"Rebecca, I never…" I try to explain but she cuts me off.

"But when my family's business and reputation are at stake, that's a whole other matter." Her eyes narrow.

"I don't think infidelity should be excused," I reply.

"You must think I'm weak," she says.

"I don't think that at all. In fact, I think it takes a strong person to keep a marriage together, especially when you're the only person in the relationship doing the heavy lifting," I explain.

Rebecca smiles sadly. "I appreciate that, but it was more of a family expectation and not wanting to rock the boat, so to speak."

"What is it that you want?"

She places her elbows on the table and leans forward. "I want to rock the boat."

She reaches down, pulls an envelope from her purse, and slides it across the table to me. I don't reach for it.

"What's this?"

"It's everything you need to take down Jonathan."

This is not how I thought this conversation was going to go.

"Infidelity can be excused. I think you're smart enough to know that politicians come back from that all the time," she says. "It's one thing for a husband to be unfaithful but quite another to commit fraud."

I look at the envelope with trepidation.

"It's not going to bite," Rebecca attempts to make a joke. "At least, not you, anyway."

"I don't want any of this to hurt you. That's why I didn't name him as a client."

"I know," she offers me a small smile, a little piece of the Rebecca I remember coming through. "I appreciate that. I already have the divorce papers drawn up and I'm taking the kids out of town for a while. Whatever you decide to do with that information, I won't be here to get pulled into the mess."

"Why are you doing this?" I ask.

"I made a mistake a long time ago." She sighs and looks down at her napkin on the table. "Merrill confided in me when she found out about Kerry and Rausch."

I stare at her in complete shock.

"I overheard you and Darren arguing last night in the hallway of the museum," she admits. "I was coming to find you." She must see the worry on my face when she says, "Don't worry, I made sure no one else overheard."

I breathe a sigh of relief.

"I made the mistake of confiding in Jonathan," she admits, and I can see the remorse written all over her face. "I didn't know he would use it against them. I'm the reason Kerry didn't run for President."

"You can't blame yourself. You're supposed to trust your husband. He's the one who betrayed you," I try to reason even though I know it doesn't help.

"I made a lot of excuses for him over the years, explaining it away as political competition and just the way things are, but my friendship with Merrill never recovered. We were cordial, but," she shakes her head. "Then she died in that horrible helicopter accident, and I never got my chance to make things right—for her and Kerry."

My heart aches for all of them. I take the envelope and slip it into my purse, clutching it to my lap as if my life depends on it. Rebecca stands, throwing cash on the table to pay for the drinks.

"You don't have to do that. Please don't leave, Rebecca," I urge her because I don't want her to leave like this when I don't know if she'll be okay.

"I have to make a flight." She then surprises me by giving me a hug. "Despite everything, I'm glad I got to know you. Darren is going to do great things, especially with you by his side," she pulls away and smiles at me. She taps on my purse that's clutched to my side. "I hope you do the right thing with this."

I watch in distress as she leaves the restaurant.

29

You're Fired

Darren

J walk through the doors of the campaign headquarters, and I'm immediately accosted by Angie, who's shoving papers into my face.

"I have the notes for the debate, and I think we should cut out the…"

I blow past her as soon as I see Rausch looking up from his computer through the glass wall of the office.

"What part of *you're fired* did you not understand?" I slam my bag on the desk.

Rausch takes his glasses off and sets them on the desk. "Darren, you fire me about once a week," he replies with annoyance.

"You gave me his address. You wanted me to find him. What did you think he would tell me?" I shake my head.

For about thirty seconds he stares at me in confusion. The minute he gets it, he stands and enters the bullpen. "Everyone out!" He orders, and they stare back at him in confusion.

"Go home. We're closing the office for the debate today."

The volunteers pack up their things, and leave. "We can discuss this calmly," he offers.

"Discuss the fact that you and my father were lovers?"

Rausch pinches the bridge of his nose, but he doesn't say anything.

"How long?" I demand.

"I'll tell you everything you want to know, but you need to calm down," he requests.

"How can I be calm, when I just found out that my whole life was a lie?" I ask.

"Your life wasn't a lie. Your parents loved you and protected you," he barks.

"Protected me from what? From knowing that their marriage was a fraud, that my mother was just his wife on paper while he was screwing around with you behind her back?" I question.

"It was not behind her back!" Rausch demands. "It's more complicated than that."

"Complicated," I say sarcastically, and I look over to Evangeline entering the office. She clutches the doorframe, looking between Rausch and me.

Rausch eyes her cautiously. "She knows," I tell him.

"Who else knows?"

"Are you afraid all the people you paid off to keep quiet will start coming out of the woodwork?" I question sarcastically. "I know you paid off my grandfather!" I bellow.

"He couldn't be trusted," Rausch demands, the vein on his temple protruding.

"You're the one who couldn't be trusted!" I yell. "Did you know my father when you were teenagers?" I accuse.

Rausch collapses into a chair. "I never hid that from you."

"Just because you omitted telling me that you grew up with my father does not give you a pass from being a liar," I demand.

"We thought it would be best if people didn't know," he responds.

I laugh. "That's why you made sure no one went digging where my father lived when he was running for office."

I smack a stack of papers off my desk and Evangeline enters further into the room. I put my hand up to stop her, and she does.

"Where do the lies end?" I request. "My mother went along with all of this?" I narrow my eyes at him and shake my head.

"Kerry would have done anything for your mother, anything to make it right. He was going to come out, but she knew if that happened, he would never go any further in his political career. It's what Merrill wanted," he explains.

"You don't get to tell me what my mother wanted," I grit out.

"I know I let you down," he offers quietly.

"You led me to him, knowing what he would tell me. Why would you do that?"

"Because I couldn't tell you!" He yells. "I wanted to. So many times, but I just couldn't," he explains.

"You're a fucking coward," I spit.

"Darren, that's not fair," Evangeline speaks up.

"No, it's fine," Rausch says to her. "I should have told you and I didn't because I couldn't take another thing from you." He casts his eyes back to Evangeline, who looks heartbroken for both of us, and it dawns on me.

"Jesus. Langley knows, doesn't he?" I look at Rausch in horror. He's been taunting me with it but I was too stupid to realize.

"Yes," Rausch answers.

I pace the room, rubbing at my jaw. "He didn't give a shit Evangeline used to be an escort when he has *this* information in his back pocket," I fume. "And you didn't tell me!" I narrow my eyes at him.

"I was handling it!"

I scoff and turn away from him.

"Was it worth it?" I ask. "You broke up a marriage and ended my father's career!"

The look of shock and hurt in his eyes makes me shudder but I'm still too angry to be intimidated.

"I loved him!" Rausch roars. "He was my everything! And now he's gone. You lost a father, and that's a horrible thing, but you are *not* the only one that has lost here."

The boom of his voice causes me to jump.

He runs a large palm over his face. "I loved your mother, too. We protected him, we guided him, we sacrificed everything, and it was all for nothing."

I don't want his tears, and I certainly don't want to feel sympathy for him.

"So, you can hate me for keeping this from you, because I deserve that," he offers. "But know that I love you like the son I never had, and it pains me deeply to know that I let you down."

I drop into the chair and lean against my thighs, palming my face. I feel the kind of tired that brings you to your knees.

"I think you should leave," Evangeline says. "Give him some time."

Rausch clears his throat. "The debate."

I close my eyes to his voice.

"Darren has to be at the community center in less than an hour."

30

Revisionist History

Evangeline

*W*e slide into the back of the car and Darren stares out the window.

"Are you okay?" I know he's not okay.

He shakes his head just as thunder rumbles in the distance. His profile is cast in shadow, and I can feel his pain like a cool slice of air.

"I can get through the debate." He crosses his ankle over his thigh and lets out a breath.

"That's not what I was asking."

He tilts his head and gives me an imperceptible nod, and then lays his head back on the headrest.

"Revisionist history," he murmurs and closes his eyes.

What do you mean?"

"We see the past the way we want to see it, not as it truly was," he explains and then grumbles, "How the fuck did I miss that?"

I lay a hand on his thigh to bring his attention back to me.

"Because we don't want to believe that we can lie to

179

ourselves. You saw your parents' marriage as impenetrable because you needed that."

"I feel betrayed in the worst way," he admits. "He gave me everything I needed to find out who he was to my father. How did he expect me to feel?"

"It was not the right way to handle it but maybe it was the only way he *could* handle it," I offer.

"I would never have expected you to make excuses for someone who treated you the way Rausch has," Darren speculates.

I let out a small laugh. "We've been at odds since the first time we met, but that's only because he loves you."

Darren whips his head at me in disbelief.

"Tell me you don't believe that?"

Darren grunts and then looks back out the window.

"I know you're not ready to forgive him, but you need each other."

He turns to me with his complicated eyes and he opens his mouth to say something, but then Bailey opens the car door.

"Darren," I lay a hand on his arm to stop him. Now is not the time to tell him about Rebecca. We stare at each other for a few moments. I want to tell him how proud I am of him, and that I believe in him, but I don't have to say any of those things out loud.

He gets out of the car, pulling me with him. "Bailey, I need you to stay with Evangeline. You go where she goes. If anyone so much as bumps into my wife…"

I interrupt him by planting my lips onto his and he yields, kissing me deeply. "You're gonna do great." I smile.

As soon as we enter the community center, the organizers descend. Angie's waiting nervously on the side of the stage.

"Is everything okay? I thought for a minute Darren wasn't coming. Where's Rausch?" She doesn't wait for me to answer while she searches around the stage.

"Darren's fine," I say, not answering her question about Rausch on purpose because I don't know, but I hope he's fine too.

She catches her breath. "I never got a chance to tell you this, but I'm sorry. I got caught up in the excitement of it all. I've never worked on a campaign before, and I just wanted to impress him. I would have never…"

I watch Darren with the organizers out on that stage, with his easy smile, and the way he holds himself with such confidence bordering on arrogance, and I know how easy it is to be caught up in his gravity.

"Okay, well, I'll just…" she doesn't finish her sentence as she hurries on stage to hand Darren his notes.

I watch from the sidelines with Bailey as they run the wire for the mic under Darren's shirt and clip it to his collar. With everything that's happened, I just now realize what he's wearing. "Shit, Bailey, his suit."

Bailey doesn't move. "I don't think he needs the suit."

Darren greets Jordie Calhoun, his opponent, who's a few inches shorter than him with dark hair and a sharp bony jaw. Bailey's right. Darren doesn't need a suit.

As seats begin to fill up, they each stand at the podium and the moderators take their seats at the table set up in front of the stage.

"Are you going to sit up front? I have seats reserved," Angie offers.

I shake my head. "No, I'm gonna stay here."

"Okay," she says, and rushes down the steps as the moderators announce the debate.

Rausch stands next to me, placing his hands in his pockets as he rocks back on his heels, and I look over at him with surprise.

"I didn't want to miss this." He positions himself behind the stage curtain, so Darren doesn't see him.

I nod.

"I don't want Darren to hate me," he says in a low voice.

"He looks up to you. You broke his trust," I explain.

"I know," his voice is remorseful.

The debate gets started. Jordie seems poised and formal, which the crowd seems to respond to. I'm biased, but I like the way Darren walks away from the podium and uses his hands when he speaks. He never liked public speaking but he's so good at it.

"Twelve percent of households in District five live below poverty level, and the median property value is two hundred and thirty-eight thousand, which tells me that your plan…"

"He does well under pressure." Rausch seems to say it more to himself than to me.

There's a loud noise. A single shot that rings through the auditorium, and there's no mistaking it for a door banging or a chair falling. A cold chill immediately blooms in my belly. Bailey grabs me, slamming me to the ground as he covers my body with his own. Rausch rushes the stage.

The auditorium erupts into chaos, people screaming as a second shot echoes throughout the community center.

"Bailey!" I yell, trying to lift my head so that I can see the stage—see Darren. "Bailey! Where's Darren? Is he okay?" I crawl a few feet across the floor towards the stage before Bailey yanks me back.

"Don't move!" he yells but I don't listen, managing to yank free from him when I see a body on the ground in front of the podium, blood blooming on his shirt, his face covered by someone frantically trying to stop the bleeding. All I can see are a pair of shiny dress shoes and I begin to cry, dropping down to my knees.

"Evan!" I hear Darren call my name as he races over, landing on his knees in front of me. "You're okay, you're okay," he grabs onto me. "Thank God you're okay." I grip him tight, and cry into his shoulder.

Paramedics arrive with a stretcher, clearing the area, and

that's when I see that it's Rausch who's been shot. Two people slide a board underneath him.

"I've got her, Bailey," Darren says, "Find out where they're taking Rausch." Bailey disappears into the crowd.

Darren grabs my hand, and we race after him. I don't know where the shooter is or if they even caught him, but all I can think about is Rausch laying on the stretcher—and there was so much blood.

"What happened?" I ask as we stop outside. On the curb is the ambulance, and they lift the stretcher into the back.

"I don't know," he says. "It happened so fast. I heard a gunshot, and then I saw Rausch run in front of me and he just dropped."

Darren's voice sounds unsteady, and his eyes are wide as he watches the paramedics close the doors to the ambulance.

"Is he…" he doesn't finish the sentence.

"I don't know," I shake my head, feeling unsteady on my feet.

"Angie?" I look around nervously to see if I can find her. People rush out of the building, most of them now milling in the parking lot. Bailey exits the side door of the community center with Angie at his side and I'm filled with relief.

"They're still looking for the shooter," Bailey explains, out of breath. "But they're taking Rausch to Inova Fairfax."

"Fuck!" Darren curses.

"What? What's wrong?" I prod him.

"That's just outside of Georgetown," he answers, and in my head, I do the math.

That's over three hours away.

"They're medevacing him from the nearest hospital. It doesn't sound good," Bailey replies.

Angie's face is white as a ghost, and she doesn't look well, but she's not hurt.

"Angie, are you okay?" I place a hand on her shoulder and that seems to focus her.

"I think so," she replies and then looks down at her body. "I'm okay."

She looks like she's in shock.

"I was just watching Darren and I heard a gunshot. It was so close it made my ears ring, and then another one. I saw Rausch running across the stage—. Is he okay?"

"We don't know," I respond.

"Angie, did you see the shooter?" Bailey asks, grabbing a nearby officer.

She nods.

"Can you describe him?" the officer asks.

"I think so," she responds, her eyes still wide. "He ran past me. It happened so fast."

"I need to get to the hospital," Darren announces. "Can you stay here with Angie?" he asks Bailey.

"I can take her to the station so she can give a statement," the officer says.

"Go," Angie comments. "I'll call my family from the station. Someone can come pick me up," she offers.

We race to the car and stop short.

"Call the pilot," Darren requests, and both Bailey and I stare at him in disbelief.

"Call the fucking pilot before I change my mind," he barks.

31

Breathe, Baby

Darren

"I'm sorry, I should have been there," Bailey says over his shoulder as he takes a sharp right towards the airfield.

"Not now," I manage to say as I start to hyperventilate.

"Breathe, baby," she soothes. "You have to breathe." But I can't.

She pushes me forward so that I'm bent between my legs and she rubs my back. "Breathe in and count to three," she instructs, and I do as I'm told. "Breathe out and count to three."

I close my eyes and I can hear the whir of the blades slicing through the air, the image of the mangled mess on the tv screen, my parents' accident, and I feel sick.

One, two, three, she counts, wiping the images from my mind until my breathing regulates.

The car stops and Bailey opens the door.

The helicopter doors are open, and the pilot is waving for me to get in, but I can't move my feet.

I look behind me to see Bailey's disheveled appearance and his apologetic eyes. "I should've done something."

I stop him, looking at Evangeline in my arms. "You were where you needed to be," I reassure him, and he nods.

"I *will* see you back in Georgetown," Bailey insists with a confidence that I wish I had.

I nod and then peer at the waiting helicopter.

"You can do this," Evangeline urges and takes my hand. "I'm right here." With those words I board a helicopter for the first time since my parents were killed.

As soon as we reach the hospital, we rush through the emergency doors and to the desk.

"Dexter Rausch, how is he?" I demand.

She looks flustered with my request but manages to pull something up on her computer.

"He was just brought into surgery. Gunshot wound to the chest, in critical condition," she fires off and my head spins.

"I want to know the minute he gets out of surgery," I demand, and feel Evangeline's hand on my shoulder.

I see the tears in her eyes and pull her further into my arms the minute she breaks down. The whole helicopter ride she was so focused on making sure I was okay that I didn't stop to think that *she* might not be.

"I'm just glad it wasn't you," she cries into my shoulder. "I'm so sorry, I just…"

"Hey, hey, I'm okay." I hold her face in my hands. The adrenaline has worn off and we both feel it.

"I'm a horrible person," she squeaks.

"You're not, you're not," I soothe. "Rausch is gonna be okay," I reassure but I don't know if that's true.

A commotion in the lobby pulls my attention and a news

crew sets up. "Jesus Christ," I let go of Evangeline and stalk over to them, but then Alistair barges into the emergency room looking appalled.

"If you have any sense, you'll take that goddamn camera and get the fuck out of this hospital!"

I've never heard him raise his voice like that before, and I'm momentarily stunned as I watch his chest heave and his face contort into someone who doesn't look like my carefree friend.

He finally notices me standing nearby and his eyes soften.

"We have every right to be here," the newswoman replies.

"You can do whatever the fuck you want but it's *not* gonna be in this waiting room," he threatens.

She finally concedes. "Let's just set up outside," she says to her cameraman.

Alistair takes two giant strides and pulls me into a hug. "How is he?"

"How did you even know what happened?" I shake my head.

"Bailey called me. He thought you might need someone."

I don't think I could love Bailey more. "We don't know anything yet," I tell him.

"Are you okay?" he asks Evangeline, who still looks shaken, but he doesn't wait for her to answer when he pulls her into a hug. She says something muffled into his neck and then pulls away, wiping at her eyes.

"Did they get the shooter?" he asks as we make our way over to the chairs.

"I don't know," I answer.

"Can I get you a coffee?" Evangeline offers.

I take her hand, pulling her down. "I just need you to sit with me."

Alistair slumps into the seat next to me.

"Thanks for being here," I tell him.

"Anything for you." He leans forward. "Both of you. You know that."

Staring at the second hand on the clock doesn't make it move any faster. The waiting room clears out, and my leg shakes with nervous anticipation as I check the clock once again.

"Why would he do that?" I shoot up from my seat and pace the waiting room because I can't sit any longer not knowing what the hell is going on in surgery.

Alistair disappears on a hunt to find a vending machine and Evangeline joins me by the window as I stare out at the rain.

She places her chin on my shoulder, and I gather her arms around my chest.

"He wanted to protect you. He always has," she replies.

"The last thing I said to him was horrible," I admit, the guilt sitting heavy on my chest.

"You were angry. You didn't know this was going to happen," she offers.

I turn around to face her and wrap my arms around her. "I can't lose another person," I admit.

"You're not gonna lose him."

The doctor comes through the double doors, and I let go of her. We both rush forward to meet him.

"Mr. Walker?" the doctor asks, his expression annoyingly unreadable.

"How is he?" I ask.

"Surgery went well. There were bullet fragments we had to remove. We just have to watch him closely for infection or fluid around the heart," he explains.

I don't know what any of that means but I focus on the part that surgery went well.

"When can I see him?"

"He's still in recovery. You can see him once we're sure

he's stable. I'll have a nurse come get you once he wakes up," the doctor replies.

Alistair returns balancing a couple of Styrofoam cups in each hand, another tucked under arm and a bag of chips between his teeth. His blond hair falls in his face and he tries to blow it out of his eyes as he makes his way over to us.

"What did they say?"

"He's out of surgery, but we can't see him yet." I relieve him of one of the cups, but I don't even know if I can drink it because my stomach is still in knots.

"Thanks," Evangeline says, taking the other cup.

"Chips?" he offers, and we both shake our heads. He shrugs, "More for me."

"You don't have to stay." He's been here for hours already and there's nothing else he can do. "We don't know when he's going to wake up."

Alistair hesitates. "Are you sure? I can stay as long as you need me."

I place my hand on his shoulder. "I really appreciate that, but we'll be fine."

Alistair nods.

"I'll call you once I hear something."

Before he leaves, he gives Evangeline another hug. "If you need anything…" he trails off, and she gives him a friendly peck on the cheek.

I lean over my thighs and hook my fingers together at the base of my neck. My whole body feels stiff.

"Maybe we should go home and try to get some sleep?"

I stretch, hearing my bones crack, and then sit back up. "I can't leave."

"Then we'll stay as long as it takes."

32

I Tripped

Darren

The waiting room is quiet at the moment and Evangeline is curled up, her head resting in my lap, when Audrina walks into the room.

"I've been,"—she pauses, noticing Evangeline asleep, and lowers her voice—"trying to get hold of you."

I pull my phone out of my pocket and notice it's dead.

"Any news?" she asks.

"Still waiting for him to wake up," I explain.

"I can't believe it. As soon as I heard I came."

"Mr. Walker?" a nurse interrupts. "Mr. Rausch is waking up. You can go in and see him now." As much as I want to shoot straight out of my seat, I don't want to wake Evangeline.

"Here, let me," Audrina holds out her sweater, folding it like a pillow, and I gently place it under her head. "It's okay, I'll stay with her. You go," she offers, waving me off.

"Thank you." I follow the nurse through the double doors and down the long hallway.

The smell and the thought of seeing him make me woozy, but I press on.

In the doorway, I watch the monitors track his heart rate and God only knows what else. His eyes are closed, and he looks fragile and small, not at all like the imposing figure he usually is—not at all like the kingmaker.

I take the seat next to his bed and put my face in my hands, trying to wipe away the weariness.

Rausch turns his head to the side and clears his throat. His voice is gravelly. "You can't get rid of me that easy, Darren."

I let out a small laugh.

"Jesus, do I look that awful?" he croaks.

"No, you look good," I lie.

"You were never a good liar, Darren," he says, turning his head straight and closing his eyes again.

"Good for someone who was just shot," I add.

I notice the pitcher of water and cup next to his bed and assume he'd be okay to drink, so I pour him a cup and offer it to him. "Here, have some water."

He opens his eyes, taking the cup from me with a shaky hand, so I try to hold it to his lips for him. "I don't need a nursemaid," he grumbles.

I look around the room. "Apparently, you do."

"Don't be cute."

"What is all this?" he fusses with the tubes attached to his chest.

"You were shot," I remind him. "And you just got out of surgery."

"I was talking about the tubes, Darren. I don't have amnesia," he grumbles and then settles back onto the pillow with a loud huff, having given up the battle.

"I was really worried about you," I admit.

"Even after all the times you tried to fire me?" he chokes out a laugh.

"I can't get elected without you," I admit.

"You don't need me." He waves me off. "You can do that all on your own."

"Is there anyone you need me to call?"

"No," he grunts and then the room settles into silence except for the steady rhythm of the monitor beeping.

"Listen, about what I said before…"

"Let's not rehash all of that," Rausch states.

"I need to say this." I let out a breath. "I was angry, and I said things I shouldn't have."

"You have every right to be angry. It's not something I should have kept from you," Rausch admits.

"I was angry because it felt like one more thing about my father that I didn't know, and you did. It's childish, I know, but I just wanted to feel like I knew him," I admit.

"You did know him. Believe me, you did," he reassures.

I rub at my jaw. "I found a letter my mother wrote to him," I explain, and Rausch turns his head to look at me. "It must have been after she found out about you."

Rausch's eyes widen, the blue a little paler than before.

"She said she'd made a decision, that she understood," I explain to him. "He kept it in *The Collected Works of Ralph Waldo Emerson*." The corners of his mouth tilt into a small smile.

"It's the same book you were reading that night I came to your house to argue about things I don't even remember now."

"You accused me of keeping information from you about Evangeline donating the money," he reminds me.

I laugh, "You have a good memory."

"I have a *long* memory," he corrects. "I know you don't want to hear this, but I was missing him that night," Rausch admits, and it makes sense now. "Reading Emerson was a way to feel close to him again."

"I'm still trying to wrap my head around all of this, to know that my whole life growing up, my parents' marriage was an arrangement, a way for my father to keep his political career while he was in love with you," I express.

"Things were different back then. People weren't as tolerant or forgiving. And you know what his family's like," he trails off.

"Is that why he decided not to run for President?" I ask.

"Langley threatened to expose him. I wanted him to run anyway, to come out in the open, but he didn't want to do that to Merrill," Rausch admits.

I run a hand along my jaw, processing all of this. "As much as I didn't want to become *that* family, under so much scrutiny—it feels like something was stolen from him."

I look up from my lap to see Rausch staring at me.

"Was my mother…?" I pause, unsure how to phrase the question of whether she was happy or not, because I'm not even sure if I want to know.

"Your father loved her immensely," he says. "He would have given up his political career for her to be happy, but she wouldn't let him. Merrill was"—he gives a small laugh, as if a memory passes through his mind—"stubborn, and loyal. Maybe too loyal. But she believed in him. We both did."

Maybe that's the answer I was looking for.

I don't want to carry this anger around with me. What happened today has put things into perspective.

"You took a bullet for me."

"I tripped."

I burst into laughter.

Rausch does the same, which dissolves into fits of coughs and sputters, causing the monitors to blare. A nurse enters the room to check on him and he tries to wave her off. She looks about as stubborn as he is but he's in no position to boss anyone around.

"I should let you sleep," I say, standing.

"You can come back and visit him in the morning," the nurse offers. "I need to take some vitals."

When she passes by, I stop her for a moment. "Is he going to be okay?"

She looks back at him fighting with the IV lines again. "There's always a risk for complications," the nurse explains, and she must see the worry in my eyes.

"Don't worry." She looks back at him and smiles. "He looks like a fighter."

I smirk, knowing how true that is.

"Darren," he calls out before I leave.

We stare at each other, and I can feel a lump form in my throat. I nod as if to say I understand, so he doesn't have to say it, and then leave the room.

When I enter the waiting room Evangeline is awake and looks to be in deep conversation with Audrina, their heads together, holding each other's hands tightly.

As soon as she notices me, she jumps from her seat. "How is he?"

"He looks good," I lie, and she purses her lips as if she can see right through me. "Ornery that he has to stay in the hospital," I add, which is the truth.

Audrina pulls me into a hug. "If I had lost you too," she doesn't get the rest of the words out, but I'm distracted by what's playing on the television above the chairs.

"What in the fuck?"

Audrina and Evangeline turn around to watch Jonathan Langley on the steps of the Capitol building commenting on the day's events as if he'd been there.

"Darren, what are you doing?" Evangeline calls after me as I head for the door.

"Audrina, stay here with her," I instruct.

"Darren!" Evangeline yells, following me out the double doors.

"I'm not going to let him use this to his advantage."

"You're emotional. I'm afraid you're going to do something stupid," she warns.

"Of course I'm emotional. Rausch almost died! Do you trust me?" I ask.

"Of course," she replies without hesitation.

"Then stay here with Audrina and let me know if you hear anything. I'll be back as soon as I can." I kiss her before I race through the parking lot and call Bailey.

The hospital is just over the Potomac and when I get to the Capitol Building, I find Langley just leaving, the camera crew packing up.

"How dare you?" I yell, stopping him on the steps.

"Ah, Darren, I'm so glad to see that you're okay. The shooting earlier was unfortunate."

"Unfortunate? Rausch almost died."

"And I hope he's recovering," Langley replies. "But I don't see why you felt the need to ambush me."

"You'll take any opportunity to spin something in your favor. You want to take credit for passing bills, but what about the ones you didn't, like gun reform, which might have prevented what happened today?"

"I didn't vote any different than my party," he argues.

"And that's the problem."

"I see you're going to make a lot of friends in Congress. That's if you can manage to get elected, the playboy son of a senator who cares more about partying than legislature," he sneers. "So don't think you can school me on policy."

"You think you can tell the public something they don't already know about me?" I ask, noticing the camera crew has set back up and it's pointing directly at us. "How's this? Yes, I was a fuckup for most of my life. I partied, got thrown out of bars, arrested for public drunkenness. I even hired an escort, which is something you can relate to, and coerced her into marrying me so I could get my inheritance."

"Your wife's press conference to gain public sympathy doesn't clean the slate for who she is. And the Virginia voters know that because they are hardworking people who understand family values, which is something I've stood for my entire career."

"What you don't know is that my wife is the most generous person you'll ever meet. She donated the five million dollars I paid her to be my wife to the Abigail Pershing Foundation, which helps thousands of battered women in the DC area. She volunteered her time and mine to serve food at a Clarksville church on Thanksgiving. You don't know about that because it wasn't for political publicity, unlike you scooping turkey for a veteran, smiling for the camera, and as soon as they were gone, so were you!" I bark.

The camera points in my direction and I take full advantage of it.

"My wife is the best thing that has ever happened to me. If it weren't for her, I would have never taken the Bar, and might I add, pass on the first try." I look at him pointedly. "She made *me* feel worthy, not the other way around, enough so that I actually thought I could make a difference in this world. *She* is the reason I'm running for the fifth congressional district in Virginia, and *she* is the reason I will win."

I turn to leave when Langley stops me. "You want to accuse me of being inauthentic? Fine. But since you're spilling family secrets, I think you're missing one." He raises an eyebrow and I know exactly what he's getting at.

"Oh, you mean the one where my father, the *late* Senator Kerry Walker, was in love with the man who just took a bullet for me?"

Langley's eyebrows shoot up.

"Or how you blackmailed my father by threatening to divulge this information so he wouldn't run for President?" The anger starts to boil over inside me and Langley's face turns red.

"You were his friend!" I point a menacing finger at him, the adrenaline running through my veins making my limbs shaky with anger.

"Those are *very* serious accusations," Langley says.

"Doesn't matter, because this is between me and you, and I'm tired of you lording this information over the people I love."

"Which is why you attacked me on the Capitol steps," he accuses.

"You wanted all this to come out anyway. I just did you a favor. And if you think I'm attacking you now then just wait until I win, because it won't be on the steps of the Capitol, it'll be on the senate floor."

"Oh, and by the way, vote for Darren Walker." I wink into the camera and then flip off Langley before I descend the steps.

My phone vibrates in my pocket, and I pull it out to five missed calls from Evangeline.

"Darren," she answers the phone with a shaky voice, and I already know why she's calling without her even saying. "It's Rausch."

I grab onto the nearby column to steady myself.

"They said there were complications," she explains, and I barely register the rest. "There was too much fluid around his heart, and the pressure caused a hemorrhage." I don't hear the rest because I drop the phone.

33

Virginia Bluebells

Darren

$\mathcal{A}$s we drive through the gates of the cemetery, the overwhelming feeling of loss washes over me. Evangeline grabs my hand and squeezes while I stare out the window, watching the headstones and the mausoleums go by until we pull alongside the curb. Bailey opens the car door, and still, I'm hesitant to get out.

"It's going to be okay. You can do this," she urges, and I give her a wan smile. *Can* and *want* are as far apart from each other as the North and South Poles.

As we walk across the soft grass, Evangeline's heels leave divots in her wake. We seem to be the only ones here, and maybe that's a good thing.

"I clipped this from the garden." She hands me a single white rose.

"The last time I was here was for my parents' funeral."

"This must be hard for you," she offers.

"Harder than I thought." I sigh as I spot the gravesite ahead.

She loops her arm through mine. I twirl the rose between

my fingers, thinking about my mother and the last rose Evangeline gave me at my parents' funeral.

I stop her before we reach the grave. "I'm sorry I wasn't there for you at your grandmother's funeral."

"You would have been there if I had let you."

"Still, I hated thinking of you there to deal with that alone. I don't know what I would have done if you weren't here with me."

"I don't want to think about the past. After everything that's happened, none of that matters anymore." She pulls me into a hug and over her shoulder I see someone approaching. She feels me tense and pulls away to track my gaze.

"Nice of you to join us," I comment once he approaches.

"I thought you'd want some time alone." Rausch shrugs and then notices the rose in my hand. "Your mother loved her roses," he smiles.

"Are you sure you're supposed be out of bed?" Evangeline inquires, a worried look on her face.

"If I spend one more minute watching reruns of The Great British Bake Off, I'm going to have a British accent."

"That or you'll be bringing in muffins for the staff," I tease.

"I think he's back to his old self."

"I don't know what you find so funny." He smoothes down his suit jacket.

I turn back to my parents' headstones and point to the bouquet of flowers in the memorial vase. "Are those from you?" I inquire.

He places his hands in his pockets and clears his throat. "Virginia bluebells," he replies. "They used to grow wild in his front yard. He told me he gave Merrill a bouquet of them on their first date," he smiles. "I thought they would like them."

"They're beautiful."

"Have you heard any news about the shooter?" Rausch asks.

"He's in custody thanks to Angie and some of the other witnesses." I glance over at Evangeline. "He's some fanatic who didn't like my *threat to family values*," I explain.

"I see." He rocks back on his heels and looks at Evangeline with regret. "I'd like to say that the world has evolved and the people with it, but I'm afraid that hasn't happened yet," he offers.

"It scares me," she admits.

"Security has been added to the events," I offer but I know it doesn't make Evangeline feel any better.

"That's the least they can do," she scoffs.

"There's a fight for another time." I turn back to the grave, still holding the rose in my hand.

"Do you want us to give you a minute?" Evangeline asks, squeezing my hand.

I nod and then kneel in front of the grave. Placing the rose on top of the headstone I say, "I'm going to be okay. You don't need to worry about me anymore."

That wasn't so bad, I say to myself, and hopefully I won't wait so long before I come back. I take a moment before I stand.

"Do you have something for me?" Rausch asks as soon as I join them.

Evangeline pulls the envelope from her purse. "Rebecca gave this to me," she explains, and the crease in Rausch's forehead deepens. "She said it was everything we needed to take down Jonathan."

"The public doesn't care how many escorts he's slept with, nor the madame that supplies them," he responds.

"It's not that," I explain.

"Oh?"

"Do you still have a contact at the Securities and Exchange Commission?" I ask.

Rausch's eyes widen. "Yes."

"I think he'd be very interested in this," I smile. "There are phone records and bank transfers among other things that implicate him in fraud with the family's hotel chain."

He lifts an eyebrow. "Rebecca is a very clever woman," he compliments. "How long have you had this?"

"She gave it to me after the charity gala," Evangeline explains.

"Jesus, why didn't you give this to me sooner?"

"Well, I was a little preoccupied with you being shot and all. I didn't even know what was in it until yesterday."

Rausch shakes his head. "You understand how this can negatively impact Rebecca," he reasons. "Are you sure you want to do that?"

"She understands what it means, and she's prepared," Evangeline responds.

Rausch takes the envelope and tucks it into his suit jacket as he looks around the cemetery.

"This could get very ugly," he advises. "Jonathan knows a lot."

I place my hands in my pocket and look at the ground. "I'm guessing you haven't seen the news or read the paper either?" I ask, skeptically.

Rausch narrows his eyes. "No, I was recovering from a gunshot wound," he exclaims, pulling his phone from his pocket.

"Didn't the doctors say you needed to keep your blood pressure down?" I speculate. "The news is never good for the heart." I try to grab the phone from him but he holds it out of reach.

I know the minute he sees the clips from my rant at the Capitol Building when his eyes grow big and the vein at his temple starts to throb. Evangeline and I are almost halfway to the car when he bellows. "Jesus Christ, Darren!"

34

Breaking News

Evangeline

"Hurry up, turn it on!" Ethel yells, and Rausch reaches to the TV on the wall and flicks it on. We all gather around in the bullpen—sitting on the desks, others on the floor, but Darren can't sit. He paces at the back of the room like a nervous father waiting for his baby to be born instead of the results for the election.

"Whatever the results, you did your best," I tell him.

"I don't like losing," he gripes.

"Oh, I know," I tease him. "But there's still so much you can do, even if you don't win."

"Remind me not to have you give a pep talk," Ethel interrupts, pursing her lips with a hand on her hip. "You're putting bad juju out into the universe," she accuses.

A Breaking News banner runs along the bottom of the screen. The room is silent while the newscaster speaks.

Senator Jonathan Langley was arrested today on charges of insider trading involving his wife's family's luxury hotel chain, Horizon Écarlate. Federal investigators allege that Langley used privileged information to benefit from stock movements tied to the

PAULA DOMBROWIAK

high-end hotel empire. The scandal has sent shockwaves through the political and business communities, raising serious questions about ethics and transparency in both spheres. Langley has denied all allegations, asserting his innocence and vowing to fight the charges vigorously.

The story was first broken by investigative journalist August Wilder of the Los Angeles Vanguard.

The room fills with chatter, and I look over at Rausch. I'd assumed he handed it to someone at *The Post* or the SEC.

"It would have been too obvious if it came from Washington," he explains with a wink.

Darren gives him a nod and we watch a clip of Langley being walked out of his home in the Kalorama neighborhood.

"Have you heard from Rebecca?" Darren asks.

"No, but I didn't expect to. She took the kids overseas until all this blows over," I explain.

"Probably for the best," he says, tugging me into his side.

The screen goes back to the regularly scheduled program, displaying all eleven districts in Virginia and the percentage of votes that have been counted so far.

"It'll be a little while before the official count is done," Darren announces. "Anyone up for pizza?" he asks the volunteers, and he gets a few grumbles. "It's on me."

Suddenly everyone starts calling out orders. "I'll call it in." Rausch excuses himself.

"I like my pizza well done and none of that pineapple or whatnot. Barbeque chicken but you tell them not to be skimpy on the chicken. You know what, hand me the phone," Ethel demands, trailing after him.

Darren grabs a hat off the desk and places it on my head, pushing it down over my eyes. "Hey," I protest, and adjust it so I can see.

He takes my hand, kissing the back of it and I look at him thoughtfully, rubbing along the stubble that lines his jaw.

"What?" he questions with a smirk.

"Nothing. I just love you."

"That's not nothing." He shakes his head, pulls me closer, and kisses me deep, leaving me longing for more.

"Is this a party or what?" Alistair barges in, setting down a bottle of whiskey.

"It's not," Darren groans, releasing me.

He inspects the bottle of whiskey and raises an eyebrow.

"Only the best for Congressman Walker," Alistair says.

"I haven't won yet," he tells him.

"Yet is the optimal word," Alistair points into the air. "And when you do, we will celebrate like kings."

True to Alistair's nature, something shiny catches his attention, and he's off, weaving through the volunteers.

I look back at the tv screen and the results are steadily coming in but still a long way off from calling a win. District eleven is still showing Calhoun ahead, which is disarming.

"There's still time. The polls haven't closed yet," I contend, trying to lift his spirits.

Darren fishes his phone from his pocket and then holds it out to me with a smirk.

Rory: Good luck, Walker.

It's just one of many encouraging texts Darren has received today from various friends and political colleagues of his father's.

As soon as the pizza is delivered, everyone descends on the boxes like a pack of wild animals who haven't eaten in days. Plastic cups of soda are passed around the room, and I can't help but feel the immense level of emotion that washes over me at the support for my husband. It's inspiring. *He's* inspiring, and I'm reminded of something Rausch said to me which feels like so long ago: *and to think, he's only scratching the surface of his potential*.

The thought fills me with both excitement and trepidation.

As the hours go by, all that's left of the pizza are crumbs and grease stains. I make myself useful by gathering them and the plastic cups that litter just about every surface of the office and take them out to the dumpster.

When I come back in, I notice Alistair leaning against Ethel's desk as she shows him the chain stitch on the blanket she's been making for her granddaughter who's having a baby.

"So, this is how blankets are made?" Alistair inspects the crocheted square.

Ethel looks at him with a horrified expression. "Boy, you're lucky God made you cute because he must have been short on smarts that day."

I snort laugh into my fist.

Alistair's head pops up, furrowing his brow at me, and I turn quickly to go find Darren.

"District five's polls are closed!" Angie yells over the chatter and we all settle down.

Darren slides into the chair next to me and his hand rests on my thigh watching the numbers come in. Across from us, Rausch rests his hands on his thighs, leaning toward the screen as if it's overtime in the Super Bowl and his team has the ball.

I feel Darren's hand clench my leg as the numbers flip: fifty-two percent Walker and forty-eight percent Calhoun. It's just skirting the line, but it's enough.

District five has been predominantly Republican, the news-caster says. *The numbers are suggesting a shift as Lynchburg begins to report results. In recent years as the district has been split, conservative democrats have been in control. This would be a first for a liberal democrat to be elected by Lynchburg voters.*

The newscaster pauses, placing a palm over his earpiece as he listens intently. *This just in. Danville has been called for Walker.*

The room erupts in cheers and back slaps.

Rausch peers at him with a proud smile.

"Doesn't matter now what Lynchburg's results are. They're gonna call it early," he explains, and I still don't understand.

As if on cue, Rausch's phone rings, and he stands. Instead of answering it, he hands it ceremoniously to Darren.

He hesitates to take it but then hits the button to answer. "Jordie," he answers with his eyes cast to the sticky, soda slicked floor. "It's Walker."

He nods and grunts and I can't take it anymore. I paw at him like a puppy looking for attention because Rausch isn't giving anything away.

"Yes, I know," Darren gives a small laugh. "It was. You too," he lets out a breath. "Thank you." He hangs up, handing the phone back to Rausch.

"Calhoun conceded!" he announces loudly, just as the news announces Darren as the winner.

The room erupts again as *Dare for Change* hats fly in the air as if it's a high school graduation, and someone opens up the dollar store confetti poppers we passed out earlier. Volunteers and staff take their turns patting Darren on the back.

He swipes a hand through his hair and looks across the aisle. Rausch holds out his hand. "Congratulations, and God help Congress," he teases.

Instead of shaking his hand, he pulls Rausch in for a hug. Rausch closes his eyes momentarily and gives Darren's back a proud slap, the sound like a clap of thunder. When he lets go, Darren gathers me up in his arms, lifting me into the air.

"We did it!" he cheers loudly and when he gently lets my feet touch the floor he says again, quietly and with deep emotion, "*We* did it."

After the last of the volunteers and staff leave, we walk back to the office to gather our things where we find Alistair sitting behind the desk, his feet propped up and a glass of whiskey in his hand.

"Our first order of business should be legalizing prostitution," he declares, wiggling his eyebrows.

"First of all, I don't have any authority over that, and second, there is no 'us'." Darren pushes his feet off the desk.

Alistair stands indignantly. "Well, as your chief of mischief affairs, I outvote you."

"There is no such title," Darren says with an annoyed tone, and I giggle.

Darren pushes him out of the office and towards the door. "This is the thanks I get for helping you get elected," Alistair says.

Darren rolls his eyes, giving him one last push out the door. "Get home safely, Alistair," Darren remarks, patting his shoulder, and then he turns to look at me with a smile that I know all too well.

"I know when I'm not wanted," Alistair bemoans with mock hurt but then his expression turns serious. "Proud of you, Dare."

Darren nods and we watch as Alistair walks to his car.

"I'm having business cards made up tomorrow. Chief of Mischief Affairs. It's happening!" He waves behind him and Darren laughs.

I like the sound of it.

Darren pulls a *Dare for Change* hat out of his pocket and places it on my head, pulling it down over my eyes again. I readjust it and give him a kiss.

"You won," I whisper against his lips.

"Oh yeah?" he grins. "Where's my prize?"

I roll my eyes teasingly. "What do you want?"

"I want you to wear this and nothing else," he commands, tapping the bill of the hat.

"Yes, Congressman." I smile.

EPILOGUE

Evangeline

I've missed the dry Arizona air and today the clouds string patterns over the blue sky, making it at least bearable to hold an outdoor press conference.

"I wouldn't be here today if it weren't for my husband, who supported this project from the minute I told him about it, and all the generous support I've received from donors," I say to a group of local news reporters and then catch Darren's eye front and center. He gives me a proud smile as he squints into the sun. "I'm proud to be able to open the first Mirabella Mitchell House for battered women, named after my grandmother, who taught me what it truly means to be compassionate."

I grab the huge pair of scissors to cut the red ribbon that's tied to both posts on the front porch. After a few tries, it finally cuts through and everyone claps.

"Mrs. Walker," one of the reporters calls out. "How many women will be moving in?"

"Great question. We renovated the house so there are eight bedrooms and two bathrooms with a shared kitchen and living room. But the great part about Mirabella House is that it's meant to be temporary, and that's why we've partnered with the Arizona Coalition for Domestic Violence."

The house has been restored back to its original beauty that I remembered from my early childhood with the help of some old photos that were left behind. There are plans to partner with local business to help the women get back on their feet and find jobs. I saw how much good Compton House did for battered women and wanted to do the same for women in Arizona.

"Will you be staying and managing the house?" someone asks.

"The house will be managed by a wonderful volunteer from the Coalition. I haven't convinced my husband to move to Arizona yet," I joke.

"Too hot!" he yells over the crowd, and they laugh.

"Does your husband have any plans to widen the scope of his political career?"

I look at Darren, and he gives me one of his wolfish grins. "He's still settling into his role, and there's still a lot of work to be done in the fifth district of Virginia," I respond.

"Would you like to see what it looks like inside?" I ask the crowd and get a unanimous yes by way of clapping.

I walk into the house with Darren while everyone else follows. The coverage this gets will help to get the word out and help our funding to grow. We've already received some great donations and grants, one of which was from Catharina Hale.

Through the crowd, I see bright red hair. "Belinda!" I give her a big hug and then notice the nice-looking older man standing at her side.

"This is my husband Bobby," she introduces us.

"So nice to finally meet you," I say, shaking his hand.

"Darren," I grab his arm and pull him over. "You remember Belinda, and this is her husband."

"I still got mace in here and I know how to use it," Belinda expresses, patting her purse with a smile.

Darren laughs nervously. "Is she always this scary?" he questions Bobby.

"No comment," Bobby offers with a laugh.

"I trained him well," Belinda whispers to me but loud enough for us all to hear.

Eddie walks tentatively into the kitchen, his hands in his pockets. "You came!"

"Well, I figured, since I donated the coffee and the pastries," he grumbles.

"I'm glad you're here."

Darren snakes his arm around my waist and pulls me into him. "I am so proud of you," he expresses.

Looking around the house, an overwhelming sadness comes over me, and Darren notices. He rubs my arms. "There's a lot of people that should be here with us today," he acknowledges, and I drop my forehead onto his chest.

I knew today would be emotional. I guess I just didn't think it would hit me so hard.

"I have the plane ready for us to leave right after this," Darren announces.

"I wish we didn't have to leave so soon," I tell him.

"Special session.' He shrugs apologetically and then releases me as one of the reporters heads in our direction.

The clouds turn a dark pink and orange as the sun sets. Darren takes my hand and leads me up the stairs of the jet. It's been a long day and I just want to sink into Darren's lap once the plane takes off and fall asleep on his chest. We get to our seats, and I see a book resting on the cushion, *A Moveable Feast*.

I pick it up and turn it over in my hand, smiling.

"Can I get you something to drink?" the stewardess interrupts.

Before I can answer, Darren suggests, "Two champagnes." He gives me a wink.

"Are we celebrating something?" I inquire.

"We have lots of things to celebrate."

I hold the book out. "I already have a copy," I explain, even though my copy is falling apart.

He smiles, running a hand through his hair.

"This one's special," he says.

"I know I ruined the other one you gave me, but you didn't have to replace it," I hold the book out to him, but he shakes his head.

"Maybe you'll want to read it on the flight," he offers expectantly with a nervous smile, and that's when I notice how odd he's acting.

The stewardess returns with two champagne flutes and sets them on the table in front of our seats. "We'll be ready to taxi shortly," she smiles.

I tuck the book under my arm and take my seat next to Darren. He reaches over and pulls my seatbelt tight. "For safety," he says.

He keeps looking at the book in my lap. "Are you okay?" I ask.

"Fine, why?" he adjusts the collar of his shirt.

"You're being weird."

"What should we toast?" he ignores me and picks up the glass, handing it to me.

I bite my lip. "To surviving being married to you," I tease.

He laughs. "How about to the opening of the Mirabella Mitchell House?"

"I will drink to that." I clink my glass with his and take a sip. He peers at me over the glass with his greenish gold eyes and dark hair falling into his face.

"You need a haircut when we get home." I push the stray pieces off his forehead.

"I've been too busy to make an appointment," he explains, and it's true.

"Ever since you won the election it's been non-stop. I feel like we've barely seen each other," I say, placing my hand on his thigh.

"Which is why we need a vacation."

"That sounds nice, but how are we going to manage that? You said you have a special session, and I have meetings," I ramble, and he places a finger to my lips.

"Aren't you going to open the book?" he requests.

"Why? Did you get Hemingway to sign it to me?" I tease. "Dear Evangeline, your husband is relentless, and I came back from the dead just to sign this book to you…"

"Don't be a smart ass," he cuts me off and I giggle.

"First editions aren't worth that much you know." I turn it over in my hand.

"That's not the point," he replies.

I roll my eyes. "Has anyone ever told you how pretentious you are?"

"Many, many, *many* times," he teases back.

I shake my head, laughing.

"Just open the damn book already," he demands.

I look at him skeptically before flipping open the cover. The pages have been hollowed out to contain a small velvet box. I close the book quickly and look over at him.

I shake my head in confusion.

Darren slides out of his seat and kneels in front of me. I can feel my chest expand and tears prick at the corners of my eyes.

"Darren?"

"Open the book," he requests quietly, and I carefully open the cover again as if there's a live bomb inside.

He takes the ring box out.

"But we're already married…"

"Just let me do it the right way this time," he says, with a nervous tremble to his voice.

He opens the box to reveal a thin antique band with a pink stone at the center surrounded by diamonds.

I put my hand over my mouth because I've never seen anything so beautiful. I play nervously with the cheap gold-plated ring he purchased from the chapel in Vegas. I've become attached to this ring.

"You didn't have to get me a new one. I like the one I have. It's special," I say, holding out my hand between us to show him.

He looks up at me with watery green eyes and I can barely contain my own tears. Sentiment threatens to unravel me.

He takes the ring out of the box and holds my hand. "It was my mother's."

The tears blur my vision and spill over onto my cheek.

"If there is one thing I know for sure, it's that my mother would have wanted you to have this," he explains, and slides the ring on my finger.

"Evangeline Walker, will you do me the immense pleasure of becoming my wife—again?" he asks with conviction.

I nod my head, unable to form the words. The seat belt prevents me from sliding out of my chair and onto his lap. I struggle to get it unclasped and once I do, I wrap my arms around him and he lifts me up.

I take his face in my hands and look into his eyes. He's my safe space, my comfort, my everything.

"Thank you," I say.

"For what?" he asks.

"For loving me the way you do."

"Is that a yes?" he asks.

"Yes," I whisper.

He runs a hand over my hair, his thumb brushing against

my wet cheek. "You've ruined me, Evangeline. There's no one else in this lifetime that could ruin me the way you have."

I kiss him with a slow and steady fervor, like the kindling of a fire that burns through me.

"If two people love each other, there can be no happy end to it," he whispers against my lips.

"Hemingway."

The door to the plane opens and Alistair barges in. "Que la fête commence!"

We both glare at him.

"Did I interrupt something?" he asks innocently.

I laugh and shake my head.

"I waited as long as I could," he explains, plopping down in one of the chairs.

"I didn't know you spoke French." I say, planting my hand on my hip.

"I am a man of many talents. Besides, I need to practice before we get to Paris," he explains and then inspects his fingernails.

I turn to Darren. "What's he talking about? And why is here?"

Darren pinches the bridge of his nose. "It was supposed to be a surprise."

He glares at Alistair.

"What?" he asks innocently.

"Are we going to Paris?" I ask Darren.

"Oui?" he answers tentatively.

"I can't believe you planned all this." I say excitedly. "But Alistair?" I whisper, giving Darren a face.

"I heard that," Alistair observes.

There's a ruckus on the stairs of the plane and then Cleo bursts through the door with her leopard print bag, holding a book in her hand. "Ugh!" she drops her bag. "Fucking traffic and some asshole cuts me off and then has the nerve to give me the finger. I thought I was gonna miss the flight," she says in a huff.

I cross the distance and give her a tight hug.

"I thought you couldn't make it to the opening of Mirabella House," I accuse and give her a friendly punch to the arm.

She shrugs. "I didn't want to ruin the surprise."

"Very sneaky, Darren Walker," I tease, and he winks at me.

"I wasn't gonna miss this wedding," she comments.

"Wedding?" I ask, looking at Darren.

"Oops." Cleo places a hand over her mouth.

"Now I know the two of you can't be trusted keeping anything a secret," Darren accuses, and both Cleo and Alistair glare back at him.

"What does she mean wedding?" I ask Darren.

He gives me a bashful smile. "I wanted to give you a real wedding and maybe convince you there is no such thing as the Paris Syndrome, because I will make sure it is everything you hoped it would be."

I think I might cry all over again. "I don't have a dress or anything."

"Already taken care of. All you have to do is show up," he smiles.

Cleo plops down in the seat next to Alistair and opens her book.

Alistair plucks it from her hands. "Is this a French transla-tion book?" he inspects it.

"Yes," she plucks it back out of his hands. "I've been studying."

"You can't learn French from a book, you have to immerse yourself," Alistair starts to explain.

"Not everyone has the luxury of skipping off to Paris and *immersing themselves* , Frenchie," Cleo exaggerates. "Besides, I took French in high school," she offers.

"Oh yeah?" Alistair lifts an eyebrow.

"The only thing I remember is voulez-vous coucher avec moi ce soir?" she says, and Alistair chokes on the glass of champagne he snatched.

"Maybe I shouldn't have invited them," Darren questions.

I laugh. "Darren Walker, if you bought me a Jessica Rabbit wedding dress I will not walk down that aisle." I would walk down that aisle wearing nothing at all if he was waiting for me at the end.

With cool confidence, he walks me towards the back of the plane where the bedroom is.

"Darren, we have guests," I laugh but the minute he opens the door, there it is and my eyes immediately well up with tears.

Inside the clear plastic bag is the most beautiful dress I've ever seen.

"It's the dress from the bridal shop in Vegas. I can't believe you remembered that."

"I remember everything," he answers, his hazel eyes holding me captive.

As he kicks the door shut behind him, I wag my finger in front of him. "Ah, ah. Not before the wedding," I tease.

"You should know by now, Mrs. Walker, I'm no virgin." He gives me that wolfish grin and picks me up in his arms.

"You know it's rude to leave your guests unattended!" Alistair calls from the other side of the door and I laugh against Darren's lips.

"Fucking Alistair," Darren groans.

Can't get enough of Darren and Evangeline? Want more of Rausch, Alistair and Cleo? If you sign up for my newsletter, you can get this bonus scene.
Use the QR Code below to access the bonus scene.

I promise I will never spam you and only send newsletters every 2 weeks. You *may* get pictures of my dog because she is extra cute and extra pampered. You *will* get exclusive information about what I'm working on, special promotions, and ARC opportunities.

ALSO BY PAULA DOMBROWIAK

THE BLOOD & BONE SERIES

A Steamy Rockstar Romance series

BLOOD AND BONE (BOOK 1)

Two days. One Interview. Twenty-five years of Rock 'n Roll. Telling his story might just repair past relationships and ignite new ones.

BREATH TO BEAR (BOOK 2)

These chains that weigh me down, my guilt I wear like a crown, SHE is my Breath to Bear

BONDS WE BREAK (BOOK 3)

To have and to hold from this day forward - to love and to cherish, till death do us part - and these are the bonds we break.

BOUND TO BURN (BOOK 4)

Love has a way of blazing through you like poison, leaving you breathless but still wanting more.

BLOOD & BONE BOXSET PLUS BONUS NOVELLA

All four books in the Blood & Bone series plus a bonus novella.

Blood & Bone legacy, bonus novella, give you a glimpse twenty years in the future through the eyes of their children.

This is their legacy.

Already read the series but just want the bonus novella?

Grab it exclusively on my SHOP

pauladombrowiak.com/shop

BLOOD & BONE LEGACY, A BONUS NOVELLA

BLOOD & BONE LEGACY

Coming in 2025

Walk the Line

Cross the Line

The Hard Line

STANDALONES

BEAUTIFUL LIES

I own the boardroom. He owns the stage. We were never meant to be together, but when somethings forbidden, it only makes you want it more.

A forbidden, reverse age gap romance

KINGMAKER SERIES

A Steamy, Marriage of Convenience, Political Romance Trilogy

King of Nothing, Book 1

Queen of Ruin, Book 2

State of Union, Book 3

ABOUT THE AUTHOR

Paula Dombrowiak grew up in the suburbs of Chicago, Illinois but currently lives in Arizona. She is the author of Blood and Bone, her first adult romance novel which combines her love of music and imperfect relationships. Paula is a lifelong music junkie, whose wardrobe consists of band T-shirts and leggings which are perpetually covered in pet hair. She is a sucker for a redeemable villain, bad boys and the tragically flawed. Music is what inspires her storytelling.

If you would like a place to discuss Paula's books, you can join her Facebook Reader Group **Paula's Rock Stars Reader Group**

You can always find out more information about Paula and her books on her website

PAULADOMBROWIAK.COM

You can also purchase eBooks, signed paperbacks, audiobooks, and multi-book bundles on her direct shop.

PAYHIP.COM / PAULADOMBROWIAKBOOKS

ACKNOWLEDGMENTS

I could not have written this book without the support of my family. Thank you so much for always being there for me, and for allowing me the space to create.

To my beautiful alpha reader's, Natalie Parker (a.k.a. Poopsie) and Mishie, I wouldn't be who I am without your friendship and this book would not be possible without your support and incredible feedback. I'm not sure how I got so lucky to call you both friends but you're stuck with me for life.

Poopsie, you saved a life. You are a true hero.

To my editor Dayna Hart, who loves to cut my word count but I'm not mad at her. She makes my stories better.

To my street team, thank you for sharing all my teasers on your social media because it makes a huge difference for this little indie author. Thank you for your friendship, and the laughs. I love you girls!!!

To all the Bookstagrammers, Bloggers, and Booktokers out there who have supported me, shared my posts, reviewed my books, and reached out to me, thank you, thank you, thank you! Word of mouth is huge! Your love of books astounds me, and I am so grateful to be a part of such a wonderful book community.

To my ARC readers, thank you from the bottom of my heart for reading and providing your honest review. Reviews are so important - especially for us little indie authors.

Last, but certainly not least, to my readers!!! I can't tell you how much you mean to me. In my heart I've always been a writer, but you make it real. I am always touched when readers reach out to me to say how much they connected with my characters. I strive to write from the heart, create characters that are real and flawed, and portray them in the most sensitive way possible. I hope you continue on this journey with me. Thank you for your support!